MY
GUARDIAN
ANGEL

SYLVIE WEIL

TRANSLATED BY GILLIAN ROSNER

SCHOLASTIC INC.

New York Toronto London Auckland Sydney
Mexico City New Delhi Hong Kong Buenos Aires

The Arthur A. Levine Books English hardcover edition was designed by Elizabeth B. Parisi and was published by Arthur A. Levine Books, an imprint of Scholastic Inc., September 2004.

ISBN-13: 978-0-439-57682-6
ISBN-10: 0-439-57682-2

Text copyright © 2001 by Sylvie Weil. Translation copyright © 2004 by Gillian Rosner.
Title page illustration copyright © 2004 by Bagram Ibatoulline.
All rights reserved. Published by Scholastic Inc. by arrangement with L'ecole des loisirs.
SCHOLASTIC, the LANTERN LOGO, and associated logos are trademarks and/or registered trademarks of Scholastic Inc.

12 11 10 9 8 7 6 5 4 3 2 1   7 8 9 10 11 12/0

Printed in the U.S.A.   40
First Scholastic paperback printing, October 2007

To Naomi and Rachel—
and for Vianne H.
on this side
of the ocean.

I

My grandfather says that all men have a Mazal: a celestial guide, a guardian angel who speaks up for them in heaven. That is what distinguishes men from animals, who, poor things, have none.

I once asked my grandfather if a girl could have a Mazal, too. At first he laughed and pinched my cheek as he always does, saying that girls don't really need the help of guardian angels, as they have no trouble speaking up for themselves! But then he grew serious and said that every single human being has one.

This means that even though there is nothing special about me, apart from being the granddaughter of the great teacher Solomon ben Isaac, I, Elvina, age twelve (nearly thirteen), have a Mazal of my own.

Perhaps my Mazal will guide me, and I certainly

hope he will speak up for me. Why? Because I am un-usual. You see, I like to write, and people say this is un-natural for a girl.

I learned to do this at the same time as my brother, Yom Tov, and my cousin Samuel. In my grandfather's house, all the women can read the Bible and write Hebrew, the sacred language of the Jewish people. It's not the custom for women to be able to do this, and some of our neighbors, Jews and non-Jews alike, point their fingers at us and stare as if we were strange. But we're used to that. My grandfather, who had no sons, saw nothing wrong with educating his daughters. If anyone disapproved, he would remind them that our Law does not forbid it.

My mother and her sisters only use this precious gift of writing to keep accounts when they go to mar-ket or to make lists of the herbs they need for their po-tions and dressings. For this, they use wax tablets.

But I, Elvina, am not content with just copying recipes or doing sums on wax tablets. What I love is to write — really write properly on parchment, using a fine quill and good-quality ink. In my grandfather's house, and in my father's house, too, no one can trim and sharpen goose quills as well as I can. My quills are fine and supple, and they don't make the ink sputter. My grandfather's students ask me for them every day.

Of course I keep some of these quills for myself. How could I bear to sharpen them with my own little knife and then dry them with such care and attention if I didn't use them? There is no pleasure, as far as I'm concerned, as great as that of filling smooth parchment with neat rows of perfectly formed letters that don't rub away like the ones hurriedly scratched onto wax tablets.

This morning I went to my beloved grandfather's cupboard and took out a piece of parchment, a well-sharpened goose quill, and some ink. I wrote down the recipe for a potion that I had just mixed by myself for the first time. To make sure the pen would glide easily and not catch, I smoothed out the parchment with my boar's tooth, a gift given to me by someone whose name I don't want to mention yet. Usually I write recipes on wax tablets, but this time the potion was a very important one. It was for my friend Tova, who is just about to give birth. The formula was complicated, and I worried that one day I might forget it. I can't depend on my mother to always be by my side to tell me such things.

Since there was some space left in the margins and at the bottom of the parchment, I added, "Elvina carefully prepared this potion on a freezing morning in the Hebrew month of Adar for her friend Tova."

I allowed my writing to stretch around the borders of the page, as I've often seen Grandfather do, so as not to waste the slightest scrap. Parchment is very expensive! So is ink — good-quality ink made with gallnuts that doesn't fade or rub out easily. Ink and parchment are reserved for writing commentaries on the sacred texts. And that is what my father, Judah ben Nathan, and my grandfather use them for.

They can't afford the fine, smooth parchment I have seen in books that rich people order from Spain. The books on which my father and grandfather write their commentaries are made with parchment that is coarse to the touch, torn in places, and patched up with rough stitches. Not all of the pages are the same shape. Some have pieces missing. Once, when I was small and didn't know much, I mentioned this to my grandfather. He laughed warmly and jokingly replied, "You think I'm a king who can afford good parchment? Mine comes from Burgundy, where the sheep are fat. Their skins may not be so fine, but they cost less and are much stronger."

I was writing along and remembering this conversation, when suddenly I heard a voice inside me cry out.

"How can you even dream of imitating Solomon ben Isaac! Who do you think you are, girl?"

Was this *you* talking to me, dear Mazal?

Oh, Mazal, Mazal, if only parchment were free, I would write you letters like the ones my grandfather dictates to me. But my letters would tell you all about *me*. I would use my best writing and tell you everything. That way, you would know me better, and you would be in a better position to stand up for me when I got into trouble.

Maybe you, too, are thinking that an insignificant little girl should not waste ink and parchment writing personal impressions that are unimportant and uninteresting. But I felt so much pleasure writing out my recipe and adding my own little sentence! I write in Hebrew characters, of course, even though I only know the names of the plants in our everyday French, the language spoken here in the land of our exile. I'm afraid that for the spelling I just have to use my imagination.

The Christians of this country write ballads that tell of the loves of gentle ladies and brave knights. Aunt Rachel adores them and has read some to me. But we Jews are only supposed to use our writing to interpret the sacred texts, as my grandfather does. People are always writing to him, often from very far away, with questions about Jewish traditions and laws.

Sometimes, when his eyes ache, he dictates one of his letters to me. I settle myself in the special high-backed armchair we use for writing, and I forget everything except Grandfather's warm, strong voice and the letters that are taking shape under my fingers.

I love to write more than anything in the world! Sometimes on my wax tablet, which I'm supposed to use for keeping accounts at the market, I start writing about something that has happened to me. I do this just for fun, but after a while I have to rub the tablet clean to write about a more recent event or to make one of my mother's shopping lists. There isn't much room on a wax tablet.

Tonight, for example, I would have loved to write you about how, at dusk, a servant rushed in breathlessly to tell my mother that Tova was feeling her first labor pains.

Immediately my mother cried out, "Quick, Elvina! Get the basket ready! It will soon be dark!"

There was not a minute to lose. Miriam, my mother, and Precious, my grandmother, were already wrapping themselves in their long, hooded cloaks. In their hands they held several little rolls of parchment tied with cord. These parchments were inscribed with verses from the Bible to ward off demons that haunt the night and others that are especially dangerous for young mothers and newborn babies. There was also an amulet containing the names of the three angels: Sanvai, Sansanvai, and Semanglof. They are the only ones with the power to protect the newborn against Lilith, the baby-snatching demon. I have heard my father and grandfather complain that we women use too many magic charms, but they have never actually forbidden us from using them.

I put everything needed for the birth into the basket, including the wolf's tooth for Tova to hang around her neck until the baby is born, and the dried agrimony with its yellow flowers, which will be tied to her thigh to ease the birth.

I added some rose oil to anoint the baby's eyelids, and a little boiled honey to smooth onto its lips. And, of course, I packed a little vial of oil mixed with essence of fenugreek, to bathe the baby's tiny, fragile body.

I carefully wrapped a piece of cloth around a bottle of my potion for Tova to drink as soon as the baby is born. I'm not yet thirteen, but all the women of

Troyes, Jewish and Christian alike, know of my skill with potions, infusions, and dressings.

You might say I've been well trained! I had barely learned to walk when my mother and grandmother began taking me with them to gather herbs from the countryside. As I grew older, they entrusted me with more difficult tasks. And yet tonight they refused to bring me along.

"But Tova is my friend!" I pleaded miserably. "She's like a big sister to me! I *must* go!"

"Certainly not!" my mother bristled. "It's dark — and you know how dangerous things are these days."

They instructed the servant to bolt and bar the door, and they bid Aunt Rachel and me good night. Then, without another word, my mother and my grandmother disappeared into the night.

II

"Aunt Rachel," Elvina whispers, "are you asleep? Talk to me! I've been lying here stiff as a corpse for hours and hours. I can't stand it any longer!"

Elvina has tried everything. She has said her prayers slowly, concentrating on every word. She has closed her eyes and kept perfectly still under the covers. But it's no good. Sleep will not come.

Usually Elvina likes to feel the coarse linen sheets against her skin through her nightdress. She likes to feel the heavy warm blankets on her body and the icy air on her cheeks and forehead. But not tonight. Tonight she feels that a century is passing, as she listens to her Aunt Rachel sniffling softly beside her and to the old servant Zipporah snoring away in the next bed as if she were gradually deflating: a loud wheeze followed by *pou-pou-pou!*

Outside, an owl hoots, as if in answer to Zipporah! The moon is almost full and shines so brightly that its light seeps through the thick canvas stretched across the narrow window. This soft, milky light should be calming and reassuring for Elvina. But tonight it neither calms nor reassures her. She coughs, turns over, and feels more and more impatient.

"Aunt Rachel," she pleads, "talk to me. I'm worried."

Aunt Rachel turns over toward Elvina and rubs her shoulder tenderly. Even when Rachel is awakened in the middle of the night, she is gentle and kind. But her face is still drowned in sleep.

"Poor Gazelle," she murmurs, her eyes still closed. "What are you worried about?"

Gazelle is the nickname Aunt Rachel gave to Elvina when she was little more than a baby, toddling after her mother and aunts as they gathered herbs in the fields. "What long legs our Elvina has," Aunt Rachel would say. "She's a real gazelle!"

"I can't get these dark, dreadful images out of my mind," Elvina wails. "I keep seeing my grandfather's troubled face. He has a deep furrow in his brow, and I'm sure it wasn't there three days ago. And my grandmother — she keeps crying and wringing her hands.

Aunt Rachel pats Elvina's shoulder. "As far as your

grandmother is concerned, I can tell you, she has never missed an opportunity to cry and wring her hands. That's just the way she is."

"But everyone seems so terrified! They drop whatever they're doing and spend the whole day plotting and planning," Elvina goes on. "My Uncle Meir rode here at top speed from Ramerupt; my father paces around, looking downhearted and anxious. Did you see the horseman who arrived in our courtyard this morning? He handed my father a few letters and rode off immediately. He didn't even dismount. His poor horse was steaming with sweat in spite of the cold. When my father and uncle finished reading those letters, they looked even more worried. Rachel, my sweet Aunt Rachel, I can see real fear written on the faces of everyone I love. If it were only the women, I could understand. But my father and my uncle! And it's not only those things I have seen that are reeling in my mind. It's also everything I've been hearing for the last two days."

Aunt Rachel stirs at last. "What have you heard?"

Elvina hugs her blanket to her chest. "I keep hearing that there are thousands of *them* spreading through the countryside like locusts. But I don't even know who *they* are!"

"*They* are the Crusaders."

"What is a Crusader?"

"A Crusader is a man who goes to Jerusalem to reclaim the tomb of Jesus from the Muslims." Aunt Rachel yawns and continues. "The pope has called on all Christians to go there and help."

"People are saying their leader is a cruel, pitiless man called Peter the Hermit," whispers Elvina. "He promises people eternal life if they follow him. And he hates the Jews."

"Don't listen to such rumors, my little Gazelle."

"He hates the Jews, and he's going to massacre us all."

"Don't you listen. . . ." Aunt Rachel's voice is almost inaudible. She yawns again and sighs. This sigh means, "Please let me go back to sleep."

Nothing ever stops Aunt Rachel from sleeping. Not her husband, who has threatened to send her back to her parents because she hasn't given him children, not Peter the Hermit's hordes who have infested the outskirts of Troyes and may at this very moment be plotting to burn down the Jewish district. Elvina resists the temptation to shake her aunt. Instead she cries out loud, "If only I were not a girl!"

"Shush . . ." Aunt Rachel murmurs. "God made you a girl. . . . He must have had a good reason. . . ."

Now Aunt Rachel is sound asleep, and Elvina feels horribly alone. She stretches out her hand and touches a small bundle under the covers near her. In the darkness she wrinkles her nose in disgust. The bundle is filled with eggs. Her mother, Miriam, has ordered Elvina to adopt them and keep them warm for three weeks until they hatch. All girls hatch eggs. It is considered a proper and profitable winter occupation for them, but for Elvina it is the height of humiliation. None of her friends can understand her attitude. Unlike Elvina, they feel love and pity for the unborn chicks and walk with motherly care to avoid shaking the eggs cradled in their aprons.

Bah! Such is the life of a girl!

If Elvina had not been a girl, she would at this very moment be across the street with her brother, Yom Tov, and her cousin Samuel. She would be in the school dormitory with all her father's and grandfather's students. The dormitory bustles with activity far into the night. If she were with the boys, she, too, would stay awake, hunched up on a mattress, wrapped in a blanket, and breathing in the acrid smoke from the pine torches. The smoke irritates your throat and makes you cough. But so what? Even though Samuel and Yom Tov are younger than she is, their lives are so much more interesting! How lucky they are to be able to spend whole nights awake, listening to the older students explaining Talmud passages from their morning class, hearing them read their notes aloud, and repeating the teacher's words. Studying keeps your mind busy and doesn't leave time for trouble to torment the soul. But poor Elvina! Even though she can read and write Hebrew better than many of the boys, she is trapped here stupidly between her Aunt Rachel and half a dozen eggs. What is she supposed to think about?

Somewhere in the distance, the convent bell tolls, calling the nuns to prayer. The familiar sound of this bell breaking the silence of the night had never disturbed Elvina before. On the contrary, she used to think the chimes sounded rather friendly. But right now, she finds them so terrifying that she cries out, "Aunt Rachel, did you hear that? It might be a signal! Maybe they're preparing to attack us!"

No reply from Rachel.

"Aunt Rachel! How can you sleep?"

Elvina leaps out of bed, slips on her thick sheepskin slippers, wraps a blanket around herself, and slips out the door.

III

Thank you, dear Mazal, thank you. You guided me to my grandfather. He blessed me. Now I can sleep.

I was sure that if I could see my grandfather, even just for a moment, I would feel much better. I knew that all the men were spending the night in the synagogue, praying but also discussing what to do about the current situation. I only hoped that Grandfather had stayed at home and was writing in his study, as he always does at night.

My parents' room was empty, and there was no one in the room downstairs. The shutter was closed, but the darkness didn't bother me. I know this house like the back of my hand. After all, I was born here. I didn't need any light to find my way to the front door and unbolt it. Outside, the night dissolved into the milky white light of the full moon. I was only going to run across the courtyard, but something made me hesitate. Never before had I ventured out of the house alone after nightfall! What if Crusaders were hiding in the henhouse or lying in wait behind the low wall where the proud cock perches to crow every morning? I strained my ears. Not a sound. So, with the blanket wrapped snugly around me, I set off.

My heart was pounding. Something jumped down from the wall. I thought I'd die of fear. I even let out a scream. It was just a cat! What a relief. He padded toward me, mewing and rubbing himself against my leg. Even so, I brushed him off sharply.

"Please, cat, now is not the time. Go away!"

Luckily, my grandparents' door was unbolted. The younger of the two servants lay curled up asleep on a pile of straw near the still-warm oven. She woke up with a start and turned toward me with puffy eyes.

"Elvina, what's wrong? What are you doing here? You know demons and ghosts come out at night!"

"Shush!" I hissed. "Don't mention such things. My grandfather says the light of the full moon is better protection than three men."

"I've heard that your friend Tova is having her baby tonight. Let's pray she doesn't give birth to a dog!"

"Don't be so stupid!" I said. "Why on earth should she give birth to a dog?"

"They say if a woman looks at a dog . . . and only last week I saw Tova stroking one. . . ."

"Leave me alone! Just go back to sleep," I shot back before she could finish.

The large room was empty and almost dark, except for a glimmer of light coming from the study. I tiptoed toward it, holding my breath. My grandfather was hunched over his table, writing. The lamp was burning gaily. It was the pretty oil lamp that my grandfather particularly likes, because you can see the flame through the glass top. Everything looked familiar and comforting. There was my grandfather, with his long gray beard dangling over the page. Now and again he brushed it out of the way with his hand.

Above him were the dark wooden shelves filled with books. I could hear the soft sound of his pen scraping on the parchment. My anxiety melted away, and my impatience flew out the window! I had turned back into the happy, carefree little girl I used to be.

I heard myself thinking, *I'll run toward him, nestle on his knee, and play with his beard. I'll touch all those pieces of parchment on the table, the big ones and the tiny ones, with letters* written all over them, up, down, and across, in every corner, so that not a single scrap of that expensive parchment should be wasted. Grandfather will get me to read words he has written. He'll take a book down from the shelves, a real book with lots of thick pages sewn together between wooden bindings. Then I'll say, "Show me your drawings," and he'll show me his plans of Solomon's Temple and the huge drawing he made of its elegant candelabrum. I will laugh at the sketches that were made in the margins by Rabbi Shemaiah, who copies down my grandfather's commentaries. There is wicked Haman with his three-cornered hat and Mordecai, as a handsome knight in chain mail. And I shall feel so proud. How many girls can boast of having the great Solomon of Troyes as their teacher! But I am, after all, his very own granddaughter.

All these things ran through my mind very quickly. And just as quickly the little voice that only I can hear exclaimed, "Elvina, stop dreaming! You are no longer four years old!"

A sudden panic seized me. What if my grandfather was angry to see me there in the middle of the night wearing nothing but my nightclothes and a blanket?

As if in answer to my thoughts, he raised his head.

"Elvina! You may be as quiet as a mouse, but I still know you are there."

"I can't sleep," I said. "I'm too worried."

"Did you cross the courtyard alone?" he asked.

"Yes."

I walked toward him. I am now too big to sit on his lap, but I took his hand and kissed it. It was icy cold from holding the pen all night, and I warmed it by rubbing it between my own hands. I wished I could also rub away the deep furrow in his forehead that I had noticed over the last few days.

Under this furrow, his warm brown eyes started to twinkle.

"It's naughty of you to have left the house, Elvina, but it's good of you to have come to warm up the heart and hands of your old grandfather, who has so many reasons to be sad tonight."

"Is it true," I asked, "that Peter the Hermit wants to kill us and burn down our houses?"

"We must pray, Elvina. We must pray, we must fast, and we must pray some more."

I had an idea. "Grandfather, isn't there a way to persuade Peter the Hermit's men to leave us in peace? I've heard that they are poor, wretched people. Maybe if we offered them food and money, we could convince them not to harm us?"

Solomon's eyes shone. "My granddaughter is very intelligent! That's exactly what we are going to do. This very night at the synagogue, your father and your

Uncle Meir are busy organizing a food collection for Peter the Hermit's troops while they are in our region. Luckily we've had a good harvest! We're going to give them vegetables, meat, and wine. . . . As for the money, once it's collected, we'll put it aside and give it to them when the time comes."

"When will the time come?"

My grandfather shook his head. "When the time comes, we'll know! You see these letters I'm writing? They are messages for our fellow Jews in Germany. We're asking them to collect money urgently to sweeten up the Crusaders once they arrive there."

"I hope they'll be gone by the time we celebrate Purim. Can we dress up and have fun as we usually do?"

I was immediately sorry I had asked this stupid, selfish question, unworthy of a girl of nearly thirteen.

My grandfather's eyebrows narrowed, and his eyes clouded over. "Who knows?" he said. "But we have to avoid anything that might be misinterpreted by our Christian neighbors. For example, we won't be burning any effigies of Haman in the street!"

I wanted to make up for my stupid question by asking another, more intelligent one. "How come Esther married a man who wasn't Jewish?" I asked.

"She had no choice. Ahasuerus was the king of

Persia, and she was his subject. Besides, her Uncle Mordecai had explained to her that the Eternal, blessed be His name, had chosen her for a special destiny. Through this marriage, she was to save the Jewish people. She was the only one who could foil the devilish plot of Haman, who wanted to massacre all the Jews. Now, go home, and go to sleep."

With these words, my grandfather took my head between his hands and blessed me.

IV

*H*er long silk dress is embroidered with gold thread; her bracelets jangle at her wrists. Her hair, twisted into thick braids, is oiled and perfumed. Her crown is so heavy with jewels that her head bends from the weight. Esther-Elvina walks slowly toward the throne room. The palace of Ahasuerus is immense, with its never-ending corridors. What will the king say when he sees that she has dared to come before him without summons? Will he rise from his throne, splendid in his royal robes of gold and precious stones? Will he take her tenderly into his arms? Or will he have her dragged outside and executed by his guards for having disobeyed his orders?

Elvina's heart is pounding. . . . The room resounds with each beat. . . . She hears the *shamash*, the synagogue caretaker, calling the faithful to morning prayers and realizes the thumping sound is really his banging on the wooden shutters. One opens and a man shouts something that Elvina cannot make out. She groans and hides her face under the covers. It isn't even day-time yet, for the cock has not crowed.

Hateful *shamash*! Horrible *shamash* whose name just happens to be Simcha, which means "joy"! He certainly *is* enjoying himself, tramping around, torch in hand, through the three streets that make up the Jewish neighborhood. What fun he has dragging everyone out of their warm, cozy beds so early in the freezing morning. Elvina stretches her arm out toward Rachel. Rachel's place is warm but empty. Elvina has the bed to herself. She thrashes her legs in all directions, those long gazelle legs that, if truth be told, she is quite proud of. She tosses and turns under the covers, stretches out luxuriously, and bumps against a small bundle. She ignores it, and with her eyes still closed, she rolls over on top of it. An awful crunch startles her awake. The eggs! She has crushed them! She imagines the disgusting little bodies of half-formed chicks making a slimy mess in the bed. The eggs are useless now; they can't even be cooked. Maybe she will manage to give them to the cats without anyone noticing. Later she'll confess to her mother.

She picks up the water pitcher and bowl that Rachel left for her, washes her hands, and says her prayers. The floor is icy against her feet. Where are those thick slippers she threw off last night? She puts on her woolen dress, quickly plaits her hair, and gathers up the shapeless squashed package, shuddering with disgust.

Downstairs her brother, cousin, and father are sitting around the table. No one sees Elvina at the bottom of the stairs. Yom Tov and Samuel are the only ones eating, hunched over a single bowl of porridge and dunking bread into it. In the silence, Elvina hears them chewing and swallowing noisily, as boys do. Rachel and Miriam are standing near the table. When Yom Tov has finally eaten enough, he turns his head toward the women with his self-important look.

"Last night I dreamed that I was walking in the country and there were wicked men who came toward me and threatened me. I was scared. Then I looked up, and I saw birds —"

Samuel interrupts him crying, "As birds fly, so will the Lord of all armies protect Israel!"

Judah ben Nathan nods his approval. "You speak well, Samuel. You have transformed your cousin's bad dream into a good one. Well done."

"I, too, had a dream," says Samuel. "I saw a horse, a magnificent white horse galloping through the forest. That's a good omen, isn't it, Uncle?"

"Yes, my son, it is."

The boys have caught sight of Elvina. Immediately they see the bundle she is trying to hide under her arm. They nudge each other, and Yom Tov cries, "You've broken your eggs again! I knew you would!"

"They are not *my* eggs. I'm not a hen! And I'd like to see you and Samuel try it. You'd break them even sooner!"

"We have more important things to do than sit and hatch eggs," they reply in unison.

"So do I!" Elvina retorts, though not very sure of herself as she feels her father's gaze turning toward her.

His harsh voice cracks like a whip. "What kind of girl are you? You know very well that in winter the hen-house is so cold that the eggs freeze, and we lose them."

"Yes, Father, I know."

Elvina wishes she could disappear underground. Anywhere to escape from the disdainful look on her father's face. "I didn't do it on purpose," she adds in a small voice.

Miriam and Rachel remain silent. Miriam looks upset, as she does whenever her husband gets angry for any reason. Elvina wonders whether, as she grows up, she will find herself adopting that meek smile she so hates to see on her mother's face.

Rachel stares at the birdcage swinging in the window. She has opened the shutter, and the birds have begun to sing. Elvina thinks they have no reason to seem so happy. The day, which has just begun, does not bode well.

No one takes any more notice of her. Judah and the boys leave the table. Miriam waits until they have gone before turning to Elvina.

"Haven't you noticed how tired and worried your father looks? Haven't you noticed he is fasting?"

"Well, that didn't stop the boys from stuffing themselves, did it?"

"They are still a long way from their Bar Mitzvah. Your father doesn't want you children to fast."

"Does he mean *me*, too?"

"Of course he does; what do you think?"

"What did he say exactly?"

"He said, 'I don't want to force Elvina or the boys to fast. They are still children and need all their strength.' Then he said, 'Why make them suffer more than necessary, when we know that hard times are on the way?'"

Rachel steps toward Elvina and strokes her hair, pressing a piece of warm bread into her hand. "Eat;

you'll feel better. I always used to break the eggs, too. Don't you remember, Miriam?"

Elvina's mother starts to laugh. "Yes. And each time you would cry, 'Poor little chicks! Poor little chicks. . . .'"

"Whereas you, Miriam, our admirable elder sister . . ."

Rachel turns back to Elvina. "Your mother never broke a single egg. I'm witness to that. She would go and see to milking the cows, she would sew, go down to draw the wine in the cellar, she would play with us all day long on the Sabbath, and those eggs never broke. Nobody knew how to keep them as safe and warm as she did. She used to wind a length of cloth around her waist to keep them secure against her body, didn't you, Miriam?"

Then Elvina starts to sob. She sobs in kind, sweet Rachel's arms. Elvina is drowning in her tears. How she wishes she could stay in Aunt Rachel's tender, comforting embrace forever, being consoled and caressed. At last she forces back her tears, raises her head slightly, and sniffs, "I hate chickens!"

Suddenly she remembers her friend. "What about Tova?"

"Tova had a little girl," says her mother. "An ugly little girl who will give her nothing but trouble!"

Miriam is grinning from ear to ear as she says this. It doesn't do to attract the attention of *mazzikim*, those demons that are always lying in wait to attack defenseless newborn babies.

"Poor Tova," says Elvina. "Her husband hoped for a boy."

Miriam laughs and kisses Elvina. "Husbands always want boys, but for mothers, it's much better to have girls! A girl is good company; a girl is a friend. You were my first child. When you were born, the neighbors all came around looking sympathetic, saying, 'Poor Miriam, how disappointed you must be.'"

"And what did you say?" asked Elvina.

"I laughed and made fun of them. . . ."

Elvina can't believe her ears. "You made fun of them? But you are always so kind and polite."

"I was younger then. I wasn't so kind in those days! But your grandfather said to me, 'Let them talk. Let them think you are disappointed. That will keep them from being jealous, and they'll wish you nothing but good.'"

V

My dear Mazal,

I can't write you, because I have no parchment, but I can still talk to you, especially because I'm all by myself, which I hate. If I had a sister instead of a brother, it would be much less lonely.

Of all the work we women have to do, what I enjoy most is spinning wool. I like the rough, slightly greasy feel of the wool between my fingers, and its warm sheep smell. I take after my grandfather in that way. When I was small, he shared with me his pleasure in the scent of the damp earth after the rain, the delicate smell of apple blossoms in the spring, and even the odor of hides being tanned. He taught me to love the pitter-patter of rain on the roof, the pale light of winter, and the silvery glimmer of the full moon. My grandfather showed me thousands of ways to find happiness in everyday things. My father is completely the opposite: He is quite indifferent to the sky, the seasons, the reflection of trees in the river, and the beauty of the world that God has created. My father is only interested in studying the sacred texts.

Meanwhile, as I ply the wool between my fingers, turning it into thread, my mind is not on my spinning. My thoughts are free to wander where they will, over to my friend Muriel's, for instance. Muriel is so lucky. She lives in a house that overlooks the street . . . and what a street it is! Her father is a furrier, and their house, which is also their shop, is right on the street where most of the Jewish shops are. She can watch the world go by, unlike me.

Today I can't even go to the younger boys' school, as I often do, to listen to them read and translate the week's lesson. The text this week is especially difficult. It's about how to make the holy robes for the high priest and how to decorate the tabernacle. It has many words that I don't know.

Dear Mazal, I know you are always watching over me, and I'm sure you are laughing to yourself now. You think I'm trying to hide something from you that you already know. Learning the vocabulary of the tabernacle is not the only reason I like going to school, but I don't want to talk about it, not even to you. Anyway, it was probably you, Mazal, who worked things out so that I couldn't go to school this morning. No, that can't be true. After all, you were not the one who built the school right next to the synagogue and the Beth Midrash where my father teaches the older boys.

One thing is certain. If I did go to school today, I might run into my father. And after this morning's scene, I don't even want to think of such a thing. The fact is, I'm scared of Judah ben Nathan, my own father, even though he has never laid a hand on me. For whenever I make him angry, he looks at me so disdainfully, I wish I could disappear through a hole in the floor.

This morning, as soon as breakfast was over, Aunt Rachel and my mother went to see Tova and her baby, for Tova has neither mother nor sister to take care of her. Before leaving the house, they gave me the same instructions I have heard over and over for the last few days: "Lock the doors. Close the shutters. And don't go out, not even into the courtyard!"

"There's plenty for you to do," my mother added. "Polish the Sabbath wine cup and tray, fold the laundry, and put it away in the chests. And there's a basket full of wool that needs spinning."

My mother was shivering in spite of her heavy

cloak and hood, and I knew in my heart that it wasn't because of the cold. No, it isn't the cold, but fear that makes us shiver this winter, for we Jews do not know what is in store for us.

I started off by polishing the Sabbath cup and the silver tray until they shone like mirrors. And I must say, I was pleased by the reflection I saw: an oval face, pink cheeks, and a fine nose that isn't red like some of my friends' noses. My hair is curly, with long, thick braids divided by a straight part. I don't have the blond braids of the ladies in the ballads, and my eyes are neither green nor periwinkle blue but more of a hazel brown. How I wish the silver tray were bigger! I have heard that rich ladies in castles have mirrors where they can admire themselves from head to toe!

Next came the laundry. What a bore! But I love the fresh scent of soap. My grandfather told me that in Germany, when he was a student, he saw women whiten their laundry by soaking it in dog dung for a day or two before washing it with soap. Every time I think of that, it makes me laugh. Maybe girls in Germany don't only have to hatch eggs but must pick up dogs' dung, too! So they are even worse off than I am!

I decided to sit and spin near the window, and despite my mother's orders, I left the shutter open.

Mazal, you do understand, don't you? How could I spend the whole day in the dark with only a little lamp for company?

The courtyard is deserted. There is not a soul to be seen unless you count the cock and the two hens that the cat chases aimlessly from time to time. They make pathetic attempts to fly off, flapping their wings in a ridiculous fashion.

The wool runs between my fingers. It runs from my left hand to my right. The staff, wedged under my left arm, gets lighter as my spindle gets heavier. I will soon have finished all my work. Ten times, I have wondered what Muriel is doing today. Ten times, I have imagined I was rushing down the street, turning the corner, and running to Muriel's without even stopping in front of the cake stall with its delicious baking smells of hot cakes and buns wafting in the air . . . without stopping at the old basket weaver's. I don't even pause at the apothecary's to glance at the flasks filled with scorpions, vipers, and toads, or the tiny scales, perfect for weighing frogs' hearts and grasshoppers' eggs! My mother and I mostly use herbs and berries that we gather ourselves. We sometimes use bark from trees and fat from cows or chickens, but once or twice I have bought leeches from the apothecary. As I sit daydreaming, I imagine the hustle and bustle of the street. I hear the merchants hawking their wares, women laughing, and children playing. I hear the spice merchant enticing me with his, "Elvina, come in here a minute; smell this cinnamon. It comes all the way from the Holy Land. It's the best remedy for tired eyes. It would be good for your grandfather, Solomon ben Isaac, who is not getting any younger, may the Lord protect him. Here, taste this ginger. Go on, do me a favor, take a few dried figs. A pretty girl like you, you'll bring me good luck."

I imagine the little donkey waiting patiently in front of the spice stall, and I see myself rubbing his ears as I eat the figs.

Mazal, who is sending me these daydreams? You, by any chance?

All I know is that I can't resist the temptation any longer. Out I go! I barely hear old Zipporah shouting out, "Elvina, where are you going? What will I tell your mother?"

"Tell her I went to take Muriel the bracelet she lent me. She wants it back."

My clogs clip-clop on the frost-hardened ground. Way up above my head, huge cotton-white clouds chase along, running much faster than I. Where are they going? When I see them race across the sky, I forget that I'm walking in the familiar narrow street of my hometown. I forget how bored I have been all afternoon. It's as if the clouds are pulling me along after them. I feel as light and joyful as they are. On my wrist I feel Muriel's bracelet. What an excellent excuse for escaping from the house!

VI

Elvina is out of breath from running. When she finally bangs on Muriel's front door, she already knows that something is wrong. The street is deserted and deadly silent, yet it is the middle of the day. Elvina can't believe her eyes. No old basket weaver, no freshly baked buns, no apothecary, and no little donkey! There is nothing, not even the sound of voices. Doors and shutters are locked, and those that are usually open to display wares are sealed tight. A few dogs scavenge through piles of rubbish, delighted that for once nobody is chasing them away.

Muriel opens the door. She looks astonished. "Didn't they tell you not to go outside?" she asks.

"Yes, but I got bored. Look, I've brought you your bracelet."

"How could you dare to leave home? Quick, come inside!"

As soon as Elvina enters, Muriel hastily bolts the door. She is with her cousins Bella, a plump dark girl of fourteen who thinks of nothing but her approaching wedding, and the twins Naomi and Rachel. The two ten-year-olds are exactly alike, with untidy wisps of curly hair escaping from their thick, dark braids. Their bright eyes sparkle with mischief, reflecting personalities to match. The four girls are busy embroidering belts and munching walnuts.

Elvina already regrets having come. "The men are all praying and fasting, and you are sitting here embroidering belts?"

"What else are we supposed to do?"

"For one thing, you could try reading this week's portion of the Torah."

Muriel gives Elvina a look that makes her blush with shame. Muriel hardly knows how to read, and her cousins, who live in a tiny village, know even less than she does. Elvina should be criticizing herself, not the other girls! What stopped her from taking out one of her father's books this morning and reading a passage from the Bible or a psalm? That might have given her some comfort. It would have been better than running to her friend's house and making spiteful remarks!

Muriel turns to her cousins. "What did I tell you? Elvina is not satisfied with her lot. She would rather be a boy and spend her life at school. When she was little, her Aunt Rachel would do her chores for her while 'Lady Elvina' learned to read and write. So now she's oh-so-proud of herself! At the synagogue, she understands when they read in Hebrew. She doesn't need to listen to the translation they read for poor ignorant folk like us. It's obvious she looks down on us."

"I don't look down on you. It's just that in *my* family women study. That's all."

Muriel is now so close to Elvina that their noses are almost touching. Her eyes narrow with anger. "You are proud, and you *do* look down on us. But you'll never find a husband. That's what my mother says."

"That depends on what kind of husband, doesn't it? I shall marry a learned man!"

"What you mean is, you won't be like Bella, who is marrying a tradesman next summer!"

"I mean nothing of the sort!"

"And you won't marry a furrier like my father, either!"

"That's not what I mean!"

"Yes, it is!"

Rachel and Naomi are standing on each side of the warring friends, keeping the score.

"Watch out; they're going to have a fight!"

"Like those two housewives I saw in the market the other day!"

Elvina looks first at one of the girls, then at the other. She sees the mischief glinting in their eyes. Suddenly laughing, she pulls their braids.

"Sorry to disappoint you, but we will not give you the pleasure of watching two girls scratching each other's eyes out and pulling out clumps of hair."

Muriel draws back, and then, in a voice dripping with honey, she meanly asks, "Where are your eggs? Have you broken them?"

The twins don't give Elvina time to answer. They each take her by the hand.

Naomi says, "This winter my mother gave us each a package of eggs for the first time. It was dreadful. We didn't dare run or even walk —"

Rachel interrupts, "But we had a brilliant idea. We put our eggs under Grandfather's blankets. He never leaves his bed. Our mother was too busy to notice, and one morning, three weeks later, Grandfather started yelling! Guess what? His bed was full of chicks!"

Naomi pulls a face. "Did we get a beating!"

The twins' sweet expressions inspire Elvina to give Muriel a kiss. "Shall we make up?" Elvina asks.

At first Muriel turns away, but then she can't help laughing along and kisses Elvina back. They have been friends forever, almost like sisters. They have quarreled and made up hundreds of times.

Elvina continues, "You guessed right. I did break my eggs, for a change. But tell me, what are Bella and the twins doing here?"

The twins are no longer laughing. In an instant, their faces seem shrunken, turning strained and pale. They huddle together and Rachel answers, "We were too scared in the village."

"The Crusaders came to our place yesterday morning and stole all of our sheep. When my father begged them to leave us at least one ewe, they pushed him so hard he fell over, and then they insulted him," Bella explains.

Naomi starts crying and Rachel joins her. Elvina takes them in her arms, strokes their tearstained cheeks, and dries their eyes with her sleeve.

"Couldn't he fight back?" she asks Bella.

"Fight back? How? You think Jews can fight back? There are thousands of Crusaders. They camp in our barns, in the forest, in the fields, on the roads. If they only steal our sheep without killing us, we can count ourselves lucky! That's what my father says."

Muriel turns to Elvina. "The streets are deserted, as you have seen, but the houses are all bursting with people. The Jews in the countryside and the outskirts of Troyes are terrified. Last night Simonet brought his wife and daughters to our Uncle Nathan the tanner's, just three doors from here."

She adds quietly, "Bella saw Peter the Hermit as close as I see you now, didn't you, Bella?"

Bella hesitates, and the twins reply for her, "She saw nothing at all. Tell the truth, Bella."

"The truth is that our elder brother spoke to someone who did see him."

Elvina is curious. "So what does he look like?"

"He looks like a donkey."

"A donkey? Are you telling me the truth, Bella?"

"Yes. His face is thin and longer than most people's. He has a filthy long gray beard, and he's barefoot and ragged — like a beggar. And he rides a donkey."

"Which looks exactly like him!" chorus the twins. They pause a second for effect, then cry, "And the donkey speaks as well as his master!"

The color has returned to their faces and their eyes are open wide, but whether in horror or in wonder it is hard to say. *Probably both*, thinks Elvina as she realizes how much she would like to have two little sisters like Rachel and Naomi, who change so easily from tears to laughter.

"What does the donkey say?" asks Elvina.

"That I can't tell you," replies Bella.

"We can!" the twins burst out. "He preaches, when his master is too tired to do it himself."

Elvina laughs. "You are just children, and people have been telling you stories. In our world, animals don't talk. In the Bible, there is a donkey that speaks to tell her master not to beat her. It is written that our Lord 'opened' her mouth. But you'll say I'm being pretentious if I tell you about it."

Naomi and Rachel draw close to Elvina. "Muriel and Bella said you were pretentious. We never did. Tell us the story of the donkey!" The twins look serious in a way Elvina has never noticed before. "Go on; tell us," they beg. "We want to know."

"It's the story of Balaam's she-ass," Elvina begins. "She told Balaam that she had always been his faithful donkey and that he had ridden her every day since boyhood, so there was no need to beat her. You see, the

Lord lent the donkey the power of speech to show Balaam that only He could decide whether a man or a beast should speak. Believe me, in our world here below, animals don't speak."

"How do you know? Maybe Peter the Hermit's donkey can."

Muriel comes to her young cousins' rescue. "That's what people are saying, Elvina. And it's not only the children."

Elvina looks thoughtful. "And this barefoot man riding a donkey is about to lead thousands of people to the Holy Land! It seems he promises them everything under the sun: forgiveness for their sins, eternal life —"

Muriel interrupts, "What if they start by burning down our homes? Have you thought of that?"

"Of course I have, just like you. But I'm not so worried, because I also think that my grandfather will find a way to avoid catastrophe. My grandfather knows everything."

VII

When I left Muriel and her cousins, I rushed home, with the sound of my clogs echoing through the empty streets. I didn't stop to look right or left. I was in such a hurry that I didn't even try to avoid the half-frozen puddles, whose dirty ice-cold water splashed me from head to toe.

At Muriel's I had pretended to be brave, but now I was overpowered with fear, especially as I arrived at the corner of our street. What if I saw a whole troop of Crusaders right in front of our house? Would I be quick enough to run in the other direction before they saw me? And what if some of them were hiding in our courtyard? Would my Mazal trouble himself to rescue me? Had I gone out against his will? In that case, would he still watch over me and get me home safely?

I was also scared I would meet my father. How

could I explain what I was doing in the deserted street? And I remembered what Bella had told me. What if those dreadful Crusaders came to our house? What if they hit my father and my grandfather as they had hit Bella's father? It was too horrible even to imagine.

But I met nobody, neither Crusaders nor my father. I only saw an old idiot beggar who drags himself along as best he can, because his legs won't carry him anymore. Still running, I shouted out to him, warning him to find shelter.

Once I was safely at home behind the barricaded door, I began to feel sad. I wondered if I really was too proud. What if Muriel was right? I *am* proud of belonging to a learned family, but her reproach had hurt me deeply. I had never heard anyone accuse my father or my grandfather of being proud, so who was I to act that way?

All this was going through my mind when I saw my grandfather crossing the courtyard. I rushed up to him and poured out my soul, telling him that I had gone to Muriel's and had been terrified on the way home and even that I had broken my eggs and that my father was angry with me. "Did God put me on earth just to hatch eggs?" I sobbed.

In spite of all his worries, he took the time to

comfort me by making fun of my silliness. He knows how to do this better than anyone.

"So," he said. "It seems my granddaughter cannot put aside the thought of those broken eggs. Believe me, your father has forgotten all about it. He has other things to worry about."

My grandfather took my hand, and we went into his house together. My grandmother welcomed us. She looked preoccupied and none too pleased. Zipporah must have told her that I had been out. Only my grandfather's warning glance stopped her from scolding me. He asked her to serve us some spicy mulled wine and then sat down, or rather collapsed, onto a bench in the downstairs room. That was when I noticed how exhausted he was, but that didn't prevent him from talking to me. He pulled his coat around himself and rubbed his hands together to warm them up. He spoke to me with affection and also seriously, as if I were not a stupid, insignificant little girl who, on top of everything else, was disobedient.

"When I was young, as you know, I studied in Germany at the famous academies of Mainz and Worms. How I loved studying! But even while I sat at my masters' feet, I was often sad, because I realized that I would not be able to study forever. I had a family to feed back here in Troyes. I have never told anyone else, but I will tell you this: It was not without shedding tears that I left my masters and returned here to look after my house and my vineyard. I was brokenhearted. Right now, you see that I am old, and you think I'm wise, but I am still nagged by regret, because I never managed to go back to Germany to visit those learned men who taught me all I know."

He smiled at me with his kindly, tired old grandfather smile. I don't know why, but this smile brought tears to my eyes, tears of warm and sweet emotion. My grandfather pinched my cheek. "You see, at the bottom of our hearts, each one of us feels sadness for the things we have left undone. But for now, come with me. I need your help."

My grandfather needed my help! I would have jumped for joy, had the serious circumstances allowed such behavior. I followed him into his study. As he handed me a fairly large sheet of parchment, he explained, "A Jewish woman had her village scribe write me to ask if she could order her non-Jewish servant to work in the fields on the Sabbath. She would like the servant to pick turnips, leeks, and other fruits and vegetables in order to prepare the meal for the end of the Sabbath. Could you reply for me? I have other letters to write."

I sat down on a stool with a board on my knees to lean on. Next to me, on another stool, I placed an inkhorn. I started writing in Hebrew:

This letter comes to you from a very young and humble member of Solomon ben Isaac's family. I have the honor of writing on his behalf and according to his instructions.

I wrote the characters in neat rows, thinking before each word, and I took so much pleasure in writing, that nothing else seemed to exist. I continued the letter:

The Law forbids you to ask your servant to work on the Sabbath, even if she is not Jewish. Your whole household has the right to rest on that day.

I had written this quite small and I still had some space left, so I added:

It is also forbidden to make your donkey, your ox, or your horse work, and you have to make sure they are well fed on their day of rest. In winter you must see that they have good, fresh hay; in the summer you should let them graze so that they can enjoy chewing the grass. Animals, too, are entitled to participate in the joy of the Sabbath.

I had wandered off the subject and lengthened the answer, so I was a little anxious when I showed my grandfather my letter. He read it slowly from beginning to end.

"I couldn't have done better, Elvina. But it does look as if you are more interested in the animals than in the servant!"

I answered that animals could not express how they felt or what they wanted and that they had no Mazal to protect them. Then I remembered Peter the Hermit's donkey.

"Is it not true," I asked, "that only man has the gift of speech?"

My grandfather's eyes sparkled. "Don't forget women and little girls!"

"For example, can a donkey talk?" I insisted. "I mean a donkey down here on earth?"

My grandfather knew immediately what I was referring to. "So you, too, have heard what they say about Peter the Hermit and his donkey? Why on earth must our own community spread such nonsense? I hope you gave your friends a sensible reply!"

"I told them that Peter the Hermit's donkey wasn't Balaam's she-ass."

"An excellent answer! I am proud of you."

Before leaving, I told my grandfather how much I enjoyed writing. How I loved to look at the words I had set down on the page, all beautifully written and arranged in neat rows. I would so have loved to be a scribe! What more wonderful occupation could there be than copying out holy texts? If only it weren't forbidden for women! How I envy those who can devote their lives to copying sacred texts on beautiful parchment! I envy Rabbi Shemaiah, who spends most of his time copying my grandfather's commentaries to make books.

Solomon ben Isaac promised me that he would give me the opportunity to satisfy my passion for writing as often as he could! For a start, he gave me three pieces of decent-sized parchment, recommending that I use them only for matters of importance.

VIII

azal, O Mazal, keep watch over your poor Elvina, who has become mistress of the house overnight, and mistress of a household of men and boys at that! My mother's heavy keys are fastened to my belt. There are five in all: two for the linen chests, another for the cupboard where we keep pots and jars of remedies. (That one must never fall into the wrong hands!) There is the key to the chest where we keep all our precious things like jewelry and silver, and, finally, there is the key to the cellar. This is the largest and most important of all, because that's where we keep the wine.

All day long, these keys jangle against one another every time I move. I hear myself coming and going as if I were my mother! But no, I am only Elvina, and I must show myself to be worthy of her confidence. That's why I'm talking to you, Mazal, as it makes me feel less alone. This house is so empty! My dear Aunt Rachel left the day before yesterday with a group of merchants on their way to Châlons. And yesterday my Uncle Meir took my mother and grandmother to his house in Ramerupt. There they will care for my Aunt Yochebed, for she is just about to give birth and she is terrified of the Crusaders.

Jews who must travel take all kinds of provisions with them to offer the Crusaders in exchange for permission to come and go. We heard that the chief Crusaders gave orders not to steal oxen or horses. For the rest, we can only hope and pray.

Before leaving, Aunt Rachel gave me a sleeveless rabbit skin tunic to wear under my dress when it gets really cold. She also gave me a pretty silver clasp to fasten my coat.

In return, I gave her my favorite amulet. It's a finely rolled piece of parchment on which, when I was small, my grandfather wrote: "The Lord is thy shepherd. The sun shall not harm thee by day, nor the moon by night."

At the last minute, just as she was about to leave the house, Rachel gave me her songbirds. "But you love them so!" I protested. "There's bound to be a corner of the cart where you can fit the cage! Those birds are your pride and joy."

"Quite so! That's why my husband says they stop me from thinking of the children I should be bearing for him. He accuses me of caring more for the birds than I do for him."

She smiled, but her eyes remained sad.

"He doesn't deserve my sweet Aunt Rachel to care for him!" I replied.

Immediately I regretted my words. Rachel burst into sobs, and so did I. We cried on each other's shoulders; then I dried her eyes with my sleeve and she dried mine with her great woolen scarf.

"How am I going to sleep all alone in the bed?" I moaned.

"Poor Gazelle! Take some more eggs; they'll keep you company!"

I pinched her and nipped her cheek. "Don't be mean!"

We laughed, then cried some more until they called us, saying that the merchants were ready to leave.

The merchants were on horseback, while boys, who must have been their sons or servants, drove the carts that were loaded up to overflowing. The carts had two horses each to pull them, so they could cover the distance quite rapidly. The men were armed with sticks and knives to ward off the usual dangers: boars, wolves, or even bandits. There is no question of trying to put up any fight against the Crusaders, though, as there are too many of them.

We helped Rachel make herself comfortable in the cart. She was squeezed between bundles of material, barrels of wine, and chickens strung together by a rope tied around their feet. They struggled and clucked while Rachel put on a brave face. "At least I won't die of starvation," she joked. "I'll try to pluck, cook, and eat one of these chickens before the Crusaders get hold of them!"

The idea that she might, in fact probably would, meet Crusaders made my heart sink. My grandmother was crying and wringing her hands. She only stopped wringing them to fasten some amulets around her daughter's neck. My mother bustled about, straightening Rachel's hood, tying her scarf, and calling to Zipporah to bring her some apples and a cake for the journey. . . .

During this time, my father spoke to the merchants, telling them which roads they should take so as not to get lost in the forest.

We watched the cart drive into the distance, taking Rachel to Châlons and to her husband, Eliezer, who certainly does not deserve her. She is so gay and good-natured that there is no one on earth who doesn't love her . . . except mean old Eliezer.

I noticed the deepening lines on my grandfather's forehead. I took his hand and asked him why Rachel was leaving the people who loved her to go back to that horrible man, who, in any case, had threatened to send her away.

"A woman's place is at home with her husband," he answered.

I replied that I would prefer not getting married at all to marrying an unkind husband. My grandfather pretended not to hear me.

Later I went with my mother to Tova's. She was no longer alone but with her cousin, who had come to join her from Ramerupt. The cousin had traveled in my Uncle Meir's wagon with all her children and two of my uncle's ewes.

As we entered Tova's house, we were overwhelmed by the stink of the asafetida. The leaves from this plant are always left burning near a newborn's cradle to keep the *mazzikim* away. I told my mother that only a demon with no sense of smell would dare come into this house, it smelled so terrible.

"Are there demons without noses?" I asked her. "I know that none of them have shadows, but do they all have noses, eyes, and ears?"

My mother put on her displeased look. "The less we mention such things, the better off we'll be," she muttered in reply.

Tova's room was fairly covered with amulets; they were everywhere, including on the bedpost and around the baby's neck. I lifted little Bellassez up in my arms. Just a few days old and so sweet! But of course it doesn't do to say so. As I hugged her, I exclaimed, "How ugly she is! Poor Tova, I'll bet she'll give you nothing but trouble!"

I laughed as I said these words, but then I added in all sincerity, "Poor little thing! What will the future bring her? Will she end up married to a mean man?"

"What a black mood you're in!" chided Tova. "I would like to think that she'll be just like you, lively and kindhearted, impulsive but generous, and always ready to admit that she is wrong."

I retorted that it wouldn't necessarily stop her from being sent back by her husband, to which my mother told me to keep quiet.

Yesterday morning it was my mother and grand-mother's turn to leave home. They set off in a big wagon pulled by two oxen. Loaded around them were cooking utensils and everything needed to help Yochebed with her baby's birth. There was plenty of food and a dozen live chickens tied together with string. These poor birds were destined to soften the hearts of any Crusaders they might meet on the way. My Uncle Meir rode his horse alongside the wagon, and there were several other men returning to the country to take care of their sheep and prune their vines. The two ewes due to lamb are staying with us. My grandfather is convinced that the Crusaders will not come all the way inside the town to steal animals. Even if they take my uncle's sheep in Ramerupt, at least he will still have these two ewes and their lambs.

As my mother and grandmother were hoisting up their skirts to climb into the wagon, I felt my throat tighten. Never before had my mother left me! I hung on to the edge of the wagon and said that I wanted to go with them, that I wanted to see my cousins, Fleurdelis, who is soon going to be six, and Isaac, who must be three by now. "I could teach them to read," I begged. "And anyway, I can help you. I promise, I'll make myself useful, indispensable even!"

My mother let go of her skirt and took both my hands in hers. And suddenly I realized that I had grown as tall as she. Our eyes were at the same level. Her eyes were red, her nose was red, too, and for a moment I had the feeling that I was the mother and she the daughter.

"Who will look after your father and grandfather, not to mention the boys? Tomorrow evening is the Sabbath. Who will prepare the table and the three meals? Who will light the Sabbath candles? Who will give the servants their orders?"

As far as giving orders was concerned, I decided to begin then and there. My grandfather's two servants and our old Zipporah were sobbing and sniffling away. Anyone would think someone had died. I sent them to get several bundles of hay, so our two travelers would be more comfortable and feel less cold.

My mother had taken the household keys off her belt and put them on mine. Then, right in front of my father, who was silently staring into the distance as if he was thinking of something else, she put on a solemn tone and began to give me instructions.

"Make sure that for the Sabbath the house is in good order. Everything in the kitchen should be in its place. The oven should be cleared of ash and filled with glowing embers hot enough to last until the next day. And see that the water compartment is filled with freshly drawn water.

"For the meal, remember, one plate per person. On the Sabbath we don't share as we do on the other days. Use wooden plates for the boys and silver for your father and your grandfather. Put the silver cup and the wine for the blessing in front of Solomon ben Isaac. Don't forget, it's your job to go to the cellar and draw the wine."

She wasn't telling me anything new. I've been preparing the Sabbath with her ever since I could walk. But yesterday, as we both stood there hand in hand, shivering, our freezing breath mingling in the cold air, I drank in my mother's words as though my life depended on it.

It was all because the little voice that I sometimes hear inside me took advantage of the fact that my mother was blowing her nose to whisper, "Soon she won't be here, Elvina. You'll have to manage by yourself. What if something happened to her, Elvina? You are a little girl no longer."

Miriam and Precious climbed up on the wagon, and they set off for Ramerupt. The oxen plodded along slowly as usual. My grandfather, my father, the servants, and I all walked along beside it. I held my mother's hand, but it was as if she had already left me. It was at that moment that my grandmother decided to give me a thousand and one instructions of her own. I knew exactly what she was going to say before she said it; I knew it all by heart. It was hard to hear her because her voice was drowned out by the chickens squawking and flapping their wings as they struggled to break free. She, too, sounded solemn. "Make sure the servants sweep the floor every evening and that they leave no crumbs," she was saying. "Crumbs bring poverty. See that there is not the slightest trace of dust on the lips of the jugs and pitchers. That also brings misery."

"Yes, Grandmother, I know."

"Don't interrupt me! In the evening, make sure you are the last to go to bed and see that the servants have left no water uncovered, because evil spirits will land on it. If one morning you find that the water has been left uncovered all night, you can use it for washing, but never let anyone drink it."

My mother patted my hand. She was smiling, and her smile meant, "You know what your grandmother's like. She'll never change!"

"Yes, I know all that, Grandmother," I said. "I'll be careful; I promise."

"I know, but I want to remind you. And see to it that not a scrap of bread is left lying around. If mice nibble it and then Samuel and Yom Tov happen to eat it, they will forget everything they have ever learned! And don't let them use their folded clothes as pillows when they fall asleep in the room after the Sabbath meal; that will also make them lose their memories!"

"Don't make such a fuss, Precious. Don't weigh Elvina down with all your instructions! Do you want her to worry herself sick the way you do?"

Solomon, my grandfather, was walking behind me. Normally, he would have interrupted Precious or just given her a look that meant "keep quiet." But this time we all knew that he was sorry to see her leave, and that he was worried, too.

We walked along beside the wagon as far as the outskirts of town. My mother was frowning in silence. She must have been going over in her mind everything she might have forgotten. Just as the wagon took the road leading to the forest, she shouted back at me. "Give Samuel and Yom Tov that old torn blanket to sit on when they go to school. It's still cold; I don't want them to catch a chill!"

When we got home, my father told me that he needed some pens. I ran to fetch two from my chest.

They were both finely shaped pens that I kept for my own use. I gave them to him. He inspected them and then said, "It seems that you have more of a gift for shaping and sharpening pens than for hatching eggs. What a strange daughter the Lord has sent me!"

He spoke gruffly, as he always does. However, I thought I heard a note of something almost friendly in his voice. Impossible! I must be mistaken!

Mazal, what do you think?

IX

It's the Sabbath and Elvina is bored! Such a thing has never happened to her before. There's nothing unusual in the fact that the weather is cold and gray and that you can't tell night from day, because it's wintertime. It's understandable that the house is dark, with the only light coming from the window in the downstairs room. That's the way it always is until the Sabbath has ended and the lamps can be lit again. But what is very strange is that Elvina is all alone in this sad, silent house with no better company than the old servant who is dozing off in the corner.

This morning, the only people in the synagogue were locals or people who have taken refuge here. The Jews from villages and hamlets outside town stayed holed up at home. There is no way they would venture out so far when hundreds of Peter the Hermit's men are on the roads!

The women's section was practically deserted. Elvina sat next to Muriel who came with her cousin Bella, the twins, and the girls' mothers, who are also twins and look exactly alike. Toward the end of the service, Elvina whispered to Muriel, "Don't leave now. Listen to my grandfather. He's going to explain the *parashah* to everyone who stays."

"You know I don't understand those things," Muriel replied.

"Oh yes, you do," Elvina insisted. "Today you'll understand. It's about how they made the *Mishkan*, the tabernacle in the desert. It's a passage that my grandfather especially likes, and when he explains it, he gives examples from everyday life. It's really interesting; you'll see."

Muriel made a face. "You think that's interesting? Carpentry and masonry? I leave those things for the boys."

"But you like jewelry, don't you? How many times have I found you in the shop next door, watching the jeweler make gold bracelets or carve patterns on silver cups? You should hear my grandfather describe the lampstand in the tabernacle and the golden cherubim with their wings spread over the ark. They kiss when

Israel is faithful to God's wishes, but they turn away from each other and cry when Israel disobeys Him. And Grandfather is bound to tell the story of the daughters of Israel in Egypt and their mirrors."

"Their mirrors?"

"Yes. They used mirrors to look attractive for their husbands. Then they became mothers and had lots of children, which explains how the Hebrews became so numerous."

The word *husbands* shook Bella out of her daydream. Elvina suddenly had her undivided attention. "What do you mean? What did they do with their mirrors?"

"They looked into them cheek to cheek with their husbands and said, 'See how pretty I am . . . much prettier than you. . . .'"

Bella burst out laughing and buried her head in Muriel's shoulder, while Muriel laughed into Bella's hair. Muriel raised her head to ask, "Did your grandfather really explain all that?"

"Oh yes, and not only to me. He told my cousin, too, and my brother. It was last night during dinner."

But despite Elvina's pleas, Muriel, Bella, the young twins, and their identical twin mothers went home with the other women, and Elvina was left all alone.

When Elvina came out of the synagogue, the narrow street outside seemed huge and empty. A lone ray of pale sunshine paused on the stone walls, turning them yellow and highlighting every detail and crack of their uneven surface. A shiver of sadness went through Elvina. It felt as if the town were deserted. There were no happy voices to be heard shouting from one house to another, none of the rich smells of meat spiced with ginger and cinnamon stewing slowly on the embers since the night before. Even the dogs had disappeared. Usually on the Sabbath day, even in winter and even in the rain and snow, the street is alive and bustling. People meet up with friends, exchange gossip, and stamp their feet to keep warm. They laugh at the clouds of steam escaping from everyone's mouth. Girls gather in tight little groups, and those from Troyes invite their country cousins home to share the Sabbath meal.

Elvina returned home as quickly as the solemnity of the Sabbath would allow. Her heavy woolen cape was gathered around her shoulders with the hood pulled down over her face. As she was about to enter the courtyard, two Christian neighbors called out to her from where they were chatting, spinning, and taking the air on their doorsteps. They stopped Elvina to ask her for news of her mother. "We never see her anymore!"

Elvina explained that Miriam and Precious had gone to Ramerupt to look after her Aunt Yochebed, who was soon to give birth. This normal conversation reassured Elvina, somewhat, that everything was just like before. She bid the neighbors good day and went home.

Later Judah and Solomon came in, followed by Samuel, Yom Tov, and several other students who have no other home but Solomon's. All of them had rings under their eyes from lack of sleep and cheeks that were hollow from fasting. None of their faces showed the joy and serenity that are usually part of this day of rest, and there was no guest with them, no merchant from afar who might fascinate all of them with tales of the faraway places he had seen. Elvina waited on Solomon and Judah with the jug and basin for them to wash their hands. Then she served the Sabbath meal on the table that she had very carefully set. She had forgotten nothing. There were several pitchers of wine, the silver cup for the blessing, and two round loaves of bread. The meat and vegetable stew she had prepared and cooked herself was delicious, spiced just right. Everyone was delighted by the excellent food.

It was a meal Elvina would always remember, because Judah asked her to sit next to him, complimenting her. "My daughter is becoming an excellent house-wife," he said. "She is indeed a worthy daughter of Israel."

Never before had he spoken to her with such a soft, gentle voice, as if he were addressing a young bride! Elvina was so dumbfounded, she didn't reply. She didn't even dare look him in the eyes. Later she regretted not having at least rewarded her father with a smile. For deep inside Elvina was very pleased and flattered. She promised herself that she would make up for her silence later on when, for the third Sabbath dish, she would serve her father and grandfather the walnuts she had fried in honey. It was Solomon's favorite sweet.

After the meal, it was time to rest. As usual, Samuel and Yom Tov lay down on the benches in the room. Elvina suddenly remembered what Precious had said to her before leaving, so she cried to the boys, "Take care, you two. Don't use your coats as pillows!"

"Oh, Elvina," they complained, "now you sound just like Grandmother!" Still, they obeyed her.

As soon as Solomon and Judah had left to return to the synagogue, though, Samuel and Yom Tov jumped up and declared that they were going for a walk.

"But we aren't allowed to go out." Elvina protested. "You heard what they said. I'm not even allowed to visit Tova."

"That's only meant for girls," retorted Yom Tov. "Anyway, we won't go far. And then we'll walk straight back to the synagogue."

She watched Samuel, the redhead, and dark-haired Yom Tov run across the courtyard. With their red cheeks to the air and their gray capes billowing behind them, they looked as if they hadn't a care in the world.

Usually on the Sabbath, the courtyard would be ringing with the happy voices and laughter of Elvina's friends and those of her mother and grandmother. This is visiting time. The house would be full of girls and women chatting, rolling apples or nuts across the table aiming to hit one another's. It's a game that Elvina thinks is a little stupid, but she is good at it. She always wins the nuts, because she can flick them more skillfully than anyone else, but she can't very well play by herself! She knows that her friends will not be coming. They, too, are forbidden to go outside.

At least Muriel, Bella, the twins, and their identical mothers have one another for company. They can tell stories while they eat honey cakes. How Elvina envies them! She would have liked to spend the afternoon with them, even if it did mean talking about dresses. Even if they called her proud. She remembers one Sabbath when her friends made fun of her because she tried to teach them to play chess. "How typical of you, Elvina," they had said. "You want to make us play boys' games. You are so pretentious!"

It would be better to talk about frivolous things with them than to be all alone in this dull, deserted room! What a wonderful occupation, sitting here by a window staring at a courtyard! In the courtyard, a solitary chicken is pecking around, and even *it* looks bored! The two ewes, after stuffing themselves with fresh hay, must have gone to sleep in the stable, because no sound is coming from them, either. Rachel's birds are twittering happily in their cage. Elvina looks out at two huge, heavy snow clouds that are wending their way slowly across the sky. What a comfortable, soft-looking sky! Elvina dozes off like old Zipporah!

Suddenly she is awakened by the panic-stricken clucking of the hen. Three men have just entered the courtyard. They are not Jews and Elvina has never seen them before. Two of them are carrying the third, a young boy whose leg is bleeding profusely. They are heading for Elvina's door. Her heart pounds so loudly that she hardly hears them knocking.

What she hears loudest of all is the servant shouting, "Don't open the door, mistress; they're sure to be Peter the Hermit's men!"

"Open the door!" Elvina orders. "One of them is wounded."

X

Tonight even old Zipporah found it hard to settle down to sleep. For the last hour I've heard her tossing and turning, moaning and imploring the heavens. She has called me at least ten times to make sure that I am really here. Where else could I be? Now, at last, she has fallen asleep.

Mazal, dear Mazal, if I could write down everything that happened this Sabbath afternoon, which I thought would be so boring, there wouldn't be room for it all on the three pieces of parchment my grandfather gave me. Anyway, I'm not sure I know how to write all the words I'd need to describe it in our holy language. And in our everyday language I don't know the spelling. It isn't a recipe, or a letter where I just have to reply to the same simple questions I've answered over and over again. What happened to me today is something that has never happened before!

No sooner had I told Zipporah to open the door than I was seized with fear. I was so scared, I felt I might faint. But I didn't. Maybe it was you, dear Mazal, who at that precise instant came down from the sky and whispered in my ear.

"Pull yourself together, girl; you only have yourself to count on!"

I stood up and faced the three men. They certainly didn't wait to be invited before entering the house and coming toward me. They were unkempt, their tunics were dirty, and their shoes and cloaks were covered with mud. The eldest of the three was the one who spoke.

"We were told that there are Jews here who know how to heal the sick. We met one in the street, but he refused to listen to us. He just mumbled something and ran away, the godforsaken dog! And what about you, girl? Have you lost your tongue?"

The rough-looking man stared at me. His pale eyes shone under bushy eyebrows. No man had ever looked at me that way, but I kept my self-control.

"I have not lost my tongue. Sit your wounded friend there, on the bench. Stretch out his leg, and take off his sock and shoe."

Among all the thoughts spinning around in my

head there was one that stood out. I remembered hearing my grandfather say that if a non-Jew's house catches fire on the Sabbath, a Jew is permitted to help put out the fire, because not doing so could have terrible consequences. Also, I must admit, I felt sorry for this wounded boy who was scarcely older than me. He was crying in pain, and I feared his wound might be dangerous. It is permitted to save a life, even on the Sabbath.

Thinking of this, I felt perfectly sure of myself. "How did your friend get injured?" I asked.

"He was trying out a sword," replied the man. "It seems he is more skillful with a pen than with weapons. Not that I can judge; I don't know how to read or write myself. All I can say is that in the Holy Land a pen is not going to be much help fighting the infidels!"

The wounded boy's two friends laughed meanly, and I tried to ignore them as I knelt down to examine the young man's wound. I sent Zipporah to fetch water, linen, herbs, an egg for the compress, and some wine for him to drink. Then, imitating my mother and grandmother, I said calmly, "Don't worry. I'm going to clean the cut and put on a dressing. It isn't very deep."

I added the last part because it's the kind of thing my mother always says to reassure her patients. In fact, the flesh was cut so deep I could see all the way down to the bone. It was white and a little shiny. I had never dressed such a gash on my own before.

Zipporah came back pale and trembling. She brought everything I had asked for, not forgetting the wine that the poor boy was in dire need of. I tried my hardest to do what my mother and grandmother would have done, starting by gently rinsing the skin around the wound. Still, I was shaking a little, rattled by the thought that if their friend's leg did not heal, they could accuse me of harming him on purpose. And then, who knows, they might come back and kill my whole family and all our friends.

As I poured a little wine on the open cut to cleanse it more thoroughly, the boy cried out, and the two men jumped toward me. I thought they were going to hit me, but they only laughed — they were always laughing — then they sat down again.

"Peter will be pleased with us," one of them said. "But believe me, we're going to have our work cut out with those two captive Jew boys. We're going to have to tame them."

"They're young," the other replied. "Once they've been baptized, they'll quiet down. I'll teach them how to use weapons; then we'll have two more Crusaders." They began to laugh again.

I was wondering who those two boys could be when suddenly I felt as though I had been punched in the chest. Where were Samuel and Yom Tov? Those young idiots had gone off for a walk in the country. Could they have fallen into the hands of the Crusaders? I leaned over the wound so the men couldn't see my face. As I was making up the compress with oil and herbs, I told myself to stay calm and, above all, not let them see that I was crazy with fear! I applied and secured the compress as slowly as I could, trying to play for time. How was I going to save my brother and cousin? Who could rescue them? What should I do?

I had absolutely no idea.

As I finished the dressing, the man with the bushy eyebrows watched me wind the clean bandages around the wounded leg.

"You wouldn't by any chance be related to the two Jew boys we captured this afternoon?" he asked slyly.

I stood up very calmly and with a steady voice I asked, "What are the two boys called?"

"One has an impossible name. The other refused to open his mouth at first, but later he told us his name was Samuel. The one with the impossible name spit at us, probably to show us how much he despised us . . . but that won't last long."

"They can't be more than ten years old," added the other man, "and they're already arrogant like all you Jews are."

Samuel and Yom Tov's fate was in my hands.

Then I had an inspiration. With much effort, I managed to grin from ear to ear. "You have captured Yom Tov and Samuel, my little brother and my cousin. I have to tell you that Samuel is an idiot child, poor thing. He understands nothing and hardly knows how to talk. He is the family's hopeless case. As for Yom Tov, whose name in our language means 'celebration,' he has a toothache so he dribbles and spits. It's not really his fault. He has too much saliva."

At that, the two started laughing again, but I must admit that this time their laughter sounded rather good-natured.

"That's enough, girl." The man with the bushy eyebrows grinned. "Your little lies don't fool us, but you have shown kindness toward our friend and we will do the same for you. We will bring back your brother and your cousin this evening. They'll get off lightly with having had the scare of their lives."

XI

hat girl could sleep after being so shaken, so frightened, and so upset? Your Elvina is so sad, Mazal. I'll tell you why, just in case you don't already know. Right now, the wind is howling and huge raindrops are beating against the canvas stretched over the window. I thank the Lord that my family and I are warm in bed, but still I can't sleep.

When my father and grandfather returned, they found me huddled in a corner, shivering with terror, still clutching the jug of wine I had served the Crusaders before they left.

Samuel and Yom Tov came back at nightfall, dirty, disheveled, and green with fear and exhaustion. They had put up a brave fight against their captors; their tunics were torn in several places. Their teeth were still chattering, but they had not been harmed.

I quickly gave them mulled wine to drink and began to tell them they should be grateful to me, but my father did not let me finish my sentence. Mazal, you know that I had played no part in their misadventure, so why did my father direct his anger at me?

"Are you never going to behave like a self-respecting daughter of Israel?" he shouted. "Are you always going to meddle with things that are none of your business?"

Finally, he told me that he was sorry he had paid me compliments earlier.

Zipporah, who was bringing in the lamps, made things worse for me by repeating at least ten times that she had tried to stop me from opening the door to the Crusaders. And poor me sitting there sniffling, stuttering that I only thought I had been doing the right thing.

Then my grandfather spoke, and according to the rules of respect toward Solomon ben Isaac, everyone fell silent. He spoke as he teaches, beginning with a question: "What is one supposed to do if a sick or wounded person arrives on the Sabbath and the person is not one of our community?" Without waiting, he gave the answer himself: "In such a case we must think carefully whether there are lives in danger.

Not only the life of the injured person, but also the lives of those on whom his companions might take revenge."

From the corner of my eye I saw my father biting his lip and fidgeting with his beard, as he does when he is displeased but unable to say anything. Solomon ben Isaac is not just his father-in-law. He is also his *teacher!* Throughout his whole life, a man remains the pupil of the teacher he has had in his youth.

My grandfather concluded, "We must be cautious, but we must also show charity." He remained silent for a few seconds, and so did we. You could have heard a fly, if there were flies in winter. My grandfather continued in a lower, sadder voice, "It is only in this way that we may avoid catastrophe."

He laid his hands on my head. "In the future, Elvina will not sit by the window when she is alone in the house. But for today, Samuel and Yom Tov owe her their gratitude."

"We would have gone to fetch them," my father said, half-protesting.

"Of course we would have gone to fetch them, but this afternoon God willed that Elvina's kindness not go unrewarded. We should all be grateful and thank the Lord. And now that the Sabbath is over, we shall recite *Havdalah*." He asked Samuel to bring the spice box and fill it up. He blessed the wine and the spices. We all smelled the spices and filled our nostrils with the warm, rich scents; then we burned them so that their perfume would spread throughout the house to comfort us for the departure of the Sabbath.

Next my grandfather lit the lamps and blessed the light. We all looked at the light through our nails and fingers. This is usually the moment when we all look at one another, relishing the pleasure of being all together and in good health. My grandfather taught us that on the evening of the first Sabbath, Adam had been terrified of the darkness. Then the Lord sent him two stones and inspired him to rub them together until sparks flew. From these sparks fire was born, and that is how Adam discovered light. "It is the light that we bless, not the lamps," says my grandfather. "And the best way to bless light is by watching it illuminate the faces of those we love." But yesterday there was no joy in our faces, even though Samuel and Yom Tov had come back to us safe and sound!

We ate, and then everyone went to bed. Zipporah unfolded a bed for the boys in the downstairs room. They were too tired to go back to the dormitory. My father went up to his room without saying a word. He didn't even wish us good night.

First Letter to the Mazal

My Dear Mazal,

My heart is heavy and my head is full of trouble, and the night has brought me no relief.

My father left as soon as Simcha, the *shamash*, knocked on the shutters. Zipporah went down to give the boys their meal. I went down, too, but I wasn't hungry. I grabbed a torch, lit it with embers from the oven, and came back upstairs to hide in my room. I couldn't possibly write you in front of the others.

My dear Mazal, I want to tell you what is on my mind. It isn't only that I have once again displeased my father. There's something else, too. Last night, I saw my father, Judah ben Nathan, worn and tired. I saw him biting his lip to keep back his words. He was displeased, but he had to hold his peace out of respect for my grandfather, Solomon ben Isaac. And it was all my fault that my father was humiliated. For once, I regretted that Solomon ben Isaac didn't pour out his wrath on me, as the Bible puts it. Can you understand that, Mazal? Do you see why I woke up with such a heavy weight on my heart?

XII

"Muriel is sick!"

The servant standing outside the door is wrapped in a cape with the hood pulled tightly over her face. Elvina can only make out one anxious-looking eye and the tip of a nose, red with cold.

"Muriel is sick!" the servant repeats.

"Don't tell me she is sick," says Elvina. "Tell me she's well."

"If she were well, do you think my mistress would have sent me out to fetch you, in the dark and in weather that even dogs avoid?"

Elvina pulls the servant inside by the arm and shuts the door. "Warm yourself up. And tell me, what's wrong with Muriel! But don't shout. It's not the sort of thing you yell from the rooftops."

The servant looks around her anxiously. "You mean that it might attract —"

Elvina finishes her sentence: "— attention. Now, tell me about Muriel."

"She's coughing and she has a fever. She was shivering all night. The mistress sent me to get you as soon as day broke or, rather, as soon as we heard the *shamash* knocking on the shutters, because it's not exactly daylight out there. . . . I followed his torchlight, and he wasn't in any hurry. It isn't enough for him to knock on the shutters to wake people up. He stops to chat, first with this one and then with that one. . . . I thought I would die of cold. But it's better to die of cold than of fright!" The servant stretches out her hands toward the fire.

At the table, Yom Tov and Samuel are finishing their meal. Three days have gone by since the Sabbath, but they have still not completely recovered from their fear, and they are eating their bread and gruel in silence. Judah has already left.

Elvina picks up the lamp.

"How are we supposed to eat?" protests Samuel.

"Open the shutter to let in a little light. How much light do you need to swallow your gruel? I need the lamp to look for the potions I'm going to take to Muriel. The jars and vials all look alike. I don't want to take the wrong ones."

A few minutes are enough to prepare her basket. Before setting out, Elvina rushes up to her room, opens her chest, and pulls out a roll of parchment on which her father had inscribed these few lines when she was little: "Thou shalt not fear the terror of the night, nor the arrow that flies by day, nor the plague that creeps in the shadows." This she ties around her neck with a string. Then she takes another parchment and hides it up her sleeve. That one is for Muriel.

Outside, it is still dark. There seems to be no separation between the earth and the sky, between the world below and that above. Everything is drowning in an icy drizzle. Elvina has her basket in one hand while the other checks that her talisman is still in place around her neck to protect her. Like the servant, she pulls her hood down over her face, and the two walk along huddled close together.

But they are not really alone. Here and there, shutters are ajar. An old woman empties a basin of dirty water into the street; another is on her way to one of the neighborhood wells, bucket in hand, head and shoulders shrouded in a blanket. Two men on their way to synagogue, their hoods up over their heads, wish them good morning.

At Muriel's house, the shutters are open. A terra-cotta lamp burns on the window ledge. Bella and the twins' mother, whom Elvina at first mistook for Muriel's, welcomes them inside. She kisses Elvina and offers her a glass of spicy mulled wine.

"Drink up quickly. This drizzle goes right through to your bones," she said. "We know that your mother and grandmother are in Ramerupt. But we also know that they have taught you their art and that sometimes you can take their place. My sister has gone to fetch water. The girls are in their room. You can go up."

The four girls are keeping themselves warm by huddling together under the covers. A wall torch sheds a dim light around the room. Muriel's face looks flushed, and she has a hacking cough.

"It's so kind of you to have come in this dreadful weather," says Bella.

Naomi and Rachel have already jumped on Elvina. "Is it true that you invited Crusaders into your house?" asks Naomi.

"Right in the middle of the Sabbath!" exclaims her sister.

"How could you do such a thing?" says Naomi.

"Didn't you die of fear?" Rachel says.

A silence falls on the room. All eyes are on Elvina. "I did what I had to do. My grandfather said I was right to do it. And yes, I did nearly die of fright."

Muriel has propped herself up against her pillows. "Leave her alone," she says in a rasping voice. "She didn't invite the Crusaders in. From what I understand, they invited themselves."

"She didn't have to open the door," says Bella.

"They might have beaten it down," says Muriel.

Rachel grabs Elvina's basket and rummages through it.

"Don't touch my basket!" cries Elvina.

"Why? Have you got frogs in there? Or scorpions?" Rachel mocks, holding the basket up triumphantly.

"Give it back!" shouts Elvina.

Elvina catches hold of the twins, and one after the other, she pinches them and tickles them, pretending to bite their soft, plump cheeks. But they run off with the basket, laughing, and Elvina once again thinks to herself that she would give anything to have two little sisters just like them, even if they always do exactly the opposite of what they are told.

"Promise us you will show us everything!" beg the twins.

"All right," says Elvina, "but why do you think I brought frogs?"

"When Grandfather was ill they put frogs on him!" Naomi replies.

Bella comes to Elvina's rescue. She takes the basket and pushes the twins back onto the bed. "You are so stupid! It wasn't frogs they used on Grandfather; it was leeches!"

"Are you going to put leeches on Muriel?" asks Rachel, wide-eyed.

"No. Sometimes my mother does that, but I don't dare. I'll do it by cupping. I need four glasses and some very hot water to heat them with. And I'll need a lamp!"

Muriel stretches out a feverish hand to Elvina. "I knew you'd come. You're such a good and faithful friend. I'm sorry I said you were proud and pretentious last time you were here."

"But you were quite right. I owe you an apology, too. Now don't talk; it'll make you cough."

Naomi and Rachel are growing impatient. "Stop all your polite talk, Elvina, and show us what's in your basket."

Opening the basket, Elvina explains, "This is syrup of poppies to calm sore throats and coughs." She produces another vial. "And this is vinegar and rosewater mixed with ashes to rub on Muriel's temples if she has a headache. And here is some sandalwood, which we will burn to purify the air in the room." She pulls the parchment from her sleeve. "And I brought a talisman."

Muriel stretches out her neck. "Tie it on for me. What does it say?"

"It's a verse from the Bible. 'All the plagues with which I have stricken Egypt, I shall not strike you with, for I am the Lord who heals you.'"

Bella and her mother bring in glasses, a jug of boiling water, and a lamp. Elvina speaks in her own mother's calm, authoritative tone: "Fill up the glasses. They have to be very hot. Muriel, lie on your stomach. Bella, pass me a glass; empty it first; just pour the water back into the jug! Quick!"

Muriel moans, "It's burning hot!"

"Don't worry! Another glass!" orders Elvina. "Get out of my light, girls; I can't see a thing!"

Lying on the bed, the twins follow Elvina's every move. "It works!" they cry out. "The skin is coming up! Muriel, does it hurt?"

"A bit." Muriel's voice is muffled in the pillow. Her back is covered with glasses under which the skin is welling up in huge red blisters.

Rachel strokes Muriel's hair, saying gently, "You are a real heroine; you'll be better in no time!"

Once Muriel is sitting up again, disheveled but looking happier, Elvina pulls one more sachet from her basket. "These are herbs my mother recommends for fever. You have to make a jug of tea every hour, leave it to cool down, and then let Muriel drink it."

As soon as their mother has left the room to go down and make the herb tea, Rachel and Naomi ask Elvina, "Isn't there a spell against the fever demon? What's his name? It's a really long one."

"Where did you pick that up from?" Elvina replies in a hushed tone.

"It's what people say. We listen; that's all."

"Well, since you are so well informed, you must know that we never mention such things aloud."

"But do you know the spell?"

Elvina doesn't reply. She has put her big cape back on, but before she has time to fasten it, the twins catch her by each hand. Their mother has taken the lamp away, but Elvina sees their eyes shining in the semi-darkness as they ask again, "You do know the spell; admit that you know it! Teach it to us; teach us the spell against the fever demon!"

"Stop it!" Elvina protests. "You're going to pull my

arms out of their sockets! I heard my grandfather mention that spell a long time ago. One of his former teachers recommended it."

"So what are you waiting for?" urge the twins.

"I can't. My grandfather does not allow that sort of thing in his house, and my father certainly wouldn't want it in his."

Rachel and Naomi won't give up. "Oh, please, Elvina, no one will know!"

"And we're not in your house!"

"Nor in Solomon ben Isaac's!"

Bella joins in, "We'll keep it secret, I promise, won't we?"

"Oh yes, yes!" they chant excitedly.

Muriel begs her, too. "Do it for me, Elvina; I'd be so grateful."

"All right." Elvina finally relents. "But let's be quick about it. Naomi, Rachel, go to the other side of the bed. Bella, come next to me." Four pairs of eyes are gazing at Elvina. "The fever demon is called Ochnotinos," she whispers.

The resin torch crackles and sputters smoke, its flame grows first bright, now dim, and the shadows dance. Bella is hanging on to Elvina's arm so tightly that it hurts. The twins are glued to each other. They are all expecting to see the wicked fever demon appear.

Elvina speaks: "We are going to shorten his name until there's nothing left of it. The demon will be very upset. He'll disappear and leave our Muriel in peace."

Naomi whispers, "He can't exist without his name, can he?"

"No demon can exist without a name," replies Elvina.

Without letting go of her sister, Rachel jumps up and down saying, "The wicked demon will get smaller and smaller. . . ."

"Repeat after me," orders Elvina. "Ochnotinos."

Bella, Rachel, and Naomi repeat, "Ochnotinos!"

"Good. Now we're going to make him smaller."

The four girls all have their eyes fixed on Elvina, who is leaning toward Muriel. The other three imitate her. Elvina takes a deep breath, then pronounces, "Ochnotinos."

"Ochnotinos," the girls echo.

"Chnotinos."

"Chnotinos."

"Notinos."

"Notinos."

"Otinos."

"Otinos."

"Tinos."

"Tinos."

"Inos."

"Inos."

"Nos."

"Nos."

"Os."

Rachel and Naomi, with their mouths shaped like Os and their round eyes full of mischief, make the "O" last as long as they can: ". . . OOOOOOOOOOOOSS-SSSSSS."

Then there is silence. "He has disappeared," Rachel whispers. "I'm sure he's disappeared. Muriel, don't you feel better?"

Muriel sits up, shakes herself a little, and smiles. "I think I do. Thank you, Elvina."

Before leaving, Elvina reminds them, "Just don't forget that you're sworn to secrecy!"

XIII

The day is still leaden and gray when Elvina leaves Muriel, but the sky has returned to its place high above the earth. Elvina pauses on the doorstep. Sniffing the air, she can make out the delicious smell of freshly baked cakes. She thinks that she may buy one. The men have stopped fasting now, for they do not want to become too weak. Her father loves these cakes and it might please him to eat one. This morning, after three days of silence, he has finally asked her if she has slept well . . . but he has also told her to go out as little as possible! The cake may not be such a good idea after all.

The street looks almost like its old self again, although there are fewer people about and less noise than usual. The women do their shopping as fast as they can and then rush home. The merchants no longer shout at the tops of their voices to attract customers.

People hold their children's hands and forbid them to wander off. The latest news is carried in whispers from one person to another: "Only yesterday the Crusaders were running high and low through the streets of Troyes." Some say there were twenty of them; others swear there were at least a hundred. The rumor goes that they were men *and* women and they hadn't thought twice about helping themselves from stalls and hen-houses belonging to Christians as well as Jews.

On the wide trestle table made from two wooden shutters, Muriel's father, Joseph ben Simon, displays a magnificent bearskin complete with its head. Elvina strokes it. "This would make a wonderful coat for this freezing weather. Without the head of course," she adds.

Muriel's father laughs. "It was a real bargain. The traveler who sold it to me was in a hurry to get rid of it and be on his way. He had killed the bear with his own hands. He was going through the forest, and the bear attacked him. Poor bear should have known better!"

Two familiar voices reach Elvina from beside the stall. "Touch the ears!" says one.

"The muzzle is even softer!" replies the other.

Rachel and Naomi are wrapped up from head to toe in blankets that are trailing along the ground. "Elvina, we followed you," Rachel says. "We didn't want to stay shut up in Muriel's room all day," Naomi adds. "We aren't the ones who are sick. We escaped. Hey, there is Uncle Nathan. He has brought out his skins as well!"

Muriel's uncle has spread several skins on the ground in front of his shop. There is a cow skin and several sheepskins whose wool has already been removed. The twins rush over and start jumping up and down on the skins. "You see, Uncle Nathan, we've come to help you."

"That's good; keep it up. The more they are trodden down, the sooner they'll be ready for tanning. They could make you a lovely pair of shoes or a saddle for a fine lady's horse."

Elvina puts down her basket and joins the twins. As she tramples on the skins, she looks upward to the heavy gray clouds scudding rapidly across the sky like battalions of soldiers. No, clouds are not like soldiers, for they carry no threat. Clouds move freely! Where are they going? Where will they be by evening? Above Paris, a city Elvina does not know, or even farther? Will they be flying over the sea, which she has never seen? How she would love to run away with them! If only she could wander freely, as they do, with the whole world unfolding below!

A slap on the back brings Elvina down to earth. She jumps in surprise. "Ouch! Naomi, Rachel! Why . . ." she begins. But when she turns around she sees neither Naomi nor Rachel.

"Marguerite!" she cries.

Under a gray hood two round rosy cheeks, blue eyes, and a smiling face can be seen. "Yes, it's me," Marguerite says. "And you, Elvina, you wicked girl, where have you been hiding? We never see you anymore!"

Marguerite is the eldest daughter of a Christian farmer for whom Solomon ben Isaac has done more than one favor. Taking hold of Elvina's cape, Marguerite shakes her playfully. "I was just talking about you this very morning with my sister Jeanne. She misses you. You used to be such good friends! What has happened?"

Elvina doesn't know what to say. For these last few weeks she hasn't had time to think about Jeanne and Marguerite. But is it really true that she hasn't had time? Not exactly. Suddenly Elvina feels boiling hot in spite of the cold piercing through her clothes. She feels so hot that sweat is pouring down her back and she turns away in embarrassment. Facing Marguerite once again, she replies quietly, "You know, we Jews don't go out much these days."

"What are you talking about? You've come out to-day, haven't you? And it seems the others have, too." Marguerite has noticed the twins eyeing her. "Tell me, Elvina, who are those little furies sticking so close to you and giving me such threatening looks?"

"They are Naomi and Rachel, Muriel's cousins. They come from the country. They don't mean to look at you that way; they just don't know who you are."

"I feel like I'm seeing double. Are they twins?" asks Marguerite with a note of fear in her voice.

When she hears Elvina's reply, she quickly crosses herself. "They say that twins bring bad luck."

"No, they don't," retorts Elvina. "It's quite the opposite, in fact!"

Marguerite gives a skeptical nod and changes the subject. "So, it seems you're afraid of the Crusaders? Why? They set up camp calmly in the fields and barns, and they don't harm anyone."

"Oh yes, they do!" shout the twins in unison. They are red with anger.

Marguerite bursts out laughing. "Your young friends are so funny. They look all ruffled up like a couple of chickens who have been chased by a dog! But I didn't mean to upset them."

Smiling, Marguerite takes Elvina by the arm.

"Listen, Elvina, I see you have your basket with you. You wouldn't happen to have a remedy for Jeanne's stomachache, would you? It would save me a trip to the apothecary."

"I have some barley water to purge her and chamomile, which will stop the pain."

"Please come over to our house," says Marguerite. "It's not far, and it would make Jeanne so happy."

Elvina hesitates. What if there are Crusaders at Marguerite's farm? She wants to refuse and say she has to go back home, but she doesn't want to offend Marguerite by looking as though she doesn't trust her. She is frightened.

While she is hesitating, she feels someone pinching her leg. Down by her feet, the old idiot beggar is grinning and laughing, dribbling into his beard. His rags hardly cover him. He drags himself over the skins toward Elvina. "You're in less of a hurry than you were the other day, little lady. Give me something from your basket. A magic potion to give my legs the strength to carry me again, so that I, too, will be able to escape when the Crusaders chase after me."

Elvina kneels down next to him. Never before has she taken the trouble to look into this man's eyes. True enough, they are crazy eyes, but, above all, they are filled with terror, even when he laughs.

For the twelve and a half years that she has been alive, Elvina has never given much thought to fear. Of course, she is familiar with the dread she feels of Judah ben Nathan's disapproval and the terror that everyone knows at the dead of night or the fear inspired by a rabid dog or the sight of a serpent slithering away underfoot in the summer fields.

But right now, Elvina is getting used to an entirely different kind of fear, which she has never felt before. She can sense this new fear all around her, and she is beginning to recognize it. The beggar, still clinging to her skirt, whines, "Please give me a remedy; the Lord will repay you. I may not look it, but I assure you, I am a worthy son of Israel."

"Are you in pain?" asks Elvina.

"My head aches as if someone was hitting me," he replies.

Elvina rummages around in her basket and pulls out a vial. "I can do nothing for your legs, but rub this ointment into your temples. It's made of ashes mixed with vinegar; it will do you good."

Marguerite is starting to get impatient. She tugs at

Elvina's sleeve, pulling her to her feet. "Come on. If you have time to care for this poor wretch, you certainly have time to visit your friend Jeanne."

Elvina kisses Naomi and Rachel and tells them to go home.

Now Marguerite and Elvina are walking quickly, their clogs clip-clopping over the ground. They have soon gone beyond the Jewish quarter, and Elvina feels uneasy. How life has changed! Only two weeks ago she would walk around in any part of this town without a second thought; after all, she was born and brought up in Troyes. This morning, however, she feels as if she is venturing into foreign territory. *Enemy territory*, she thinks to herself. Just this morning Judah ben Nathan has begun to speak to her again! If he finds out about this latest adventure, he will be displeased once more! But does she have a choice?

Marguerite, still holding on to Elvina's arm, throws her a mischievous glance. "I heard that the other day you took care of a young Crusader called Gauthier. He's good-looking, don't you think?"

"I have no idea," replies Elvina, trying to sound calm.

"Am I supposed to think that you looked at nothing but his leg?" hints Marguerite.

"I was terrified! They had captured Samuel and Yom Tov."

"They only did it for a laugh," replies Marguerite. "You take these things too seriously."

Elvina does not reply. Her heart is beating so hard that she feels certain Marguerite must hear it. She tells herself to calm down. After all, Marguerite is sweet-natured and kind, even if she does like a joke. The voice inside Elvina continues, trying to reassure her. *You can stay at their house just a few minutes — long enough to say hello to Jeanne. There's nothing to be afraid of.*

XIV

arguerite's house stands on a large farm-yard. Clucking hens run hither and thither, and grunting pigs root around in a pile of rubbish. Marguerite's mother and the servant are stacking logs and kindling, their skirts gathered up in their belts. Two geese cackle threateningly toward Elvina, their open beaks ready to bite. Elvina has a hard time pushing them away. She swings her basket at them, but they duck their long necks to avoid it, then stretch up again and come rushing back at her. Marguerite's mother and the servant have stopped their work to observe the scene. They are screaming with laughter. "Do our geese scare you, Elvina?"

"Your geese are worse than dogs!" Elvina retorts.

The two women stand with their hands on their hips and laugh harder. "They don't recognize you any-more," jokes Marguerite's mother. "It isn't nice to neglect us so, especially since you have always been at home on our farm. Jeanne will give you some fresh curd cheese; we have two big pots full. And if you fancy it, you can drink some of the whey. I remember how much you liked that when you were little. Tell me, is your grandfather, Solomon ben Isaac, in good health?"

"He's fine, thank God."

"I'm glad to hear it. We haven't seen him for a long time, and we miss him." Marguerite's mother has a pleasant voice. Some of her front teeth are missing, and this gives her a slight lisp, which adds to the softness of her speech.

Elvina's anxiety melts away. She no longer sees any reason to hurry. The faces around her are familiar and reassuring, and there is no trace of Crusaders. The farmer's family is making her feel welcome; they have asked about her grandfather and are offering her the whey she loves to drink so much. It is as if nothing has ever happened, as if Peter the Hermit, the Crusaders, and all the fear has been just a bad dream. Here life goes on as usual, with its background of peaceful grunting pigs, hissing geese, and clucking hens.

Marguerite has already rushed into the house. "Jeanne, Jeanne, guess who I've brought home? Your friend Elvina!"

"Elvina! I'm so happy!" Jeanne cries.

Inside, the room is as hot and dark as an oven. Jeanne runs over to Elvina and hugs her. She is holding a long willow stem. "Come and see the pretty baskets Marie and I are weaving."

In the darkness, Elvina can hardly make out Marie, the youngest of the three sisters, who is kneeling next to the stove. Marie nods at Elvina without putting down her work. Near her on a stool stands a terra-cotta lamp, its flame flickering and spluttering as if it might go out at any minute. Jeanne leads Elvina close to the stove, where there is a roaring fire.

"You have come to visit us on a day that is hardly better than the night. We lit the lamp, but the wick won't burn as it should; it only gives out a tiny bit of light and we have to weave our baskets by feel, as if we were blind!"

"Do you have any salt?" Elvina asks her friend.

"Of course we do!" answers Marguerite.

"Bring me a pinch."

The three sisters watch Elvina as she cautiously lifts the cover of the lamp and throws the salt into the hollow that contains the oil. Immediately the wick catches and a bright flame appears. "There you are!" cries Elvina triumphantly.

She turns around to face her friends, delighted at her success. Their silence and the expression on their now clearly visible faces turn her blood to ice. She forces herself to keep smiling. "Aren't you pleased? You are looking at me as if you've never set eyes upon me before! What's the matter?"

"The matter is that we find witchcraft scary," replies Marguerite.

"What witchcraft?" asks Elvina in disbelief. "That's not witchcraft! The salt clears the oil, so the wick catches more easily and burns with a stronger flame. My grandfather taught me that when I was small. It's in our books."

Jeanne stands directly in front of Elvina and takes her by the shoulders. "That's just it," she begins accusingly. "Those books of yours. You said it yourself. My cousin, the priest, told us all about them. You Jews always have your heads bent over those big books of yours because they give you special powers. And of course you don't want to give them up, and that's why you're so frightened of the Crusaders. If you would only get baptized and give up your books, you could be just like everyone else."

"But we *are* like everyone else!" cries Elvina, scarcely able to believe her ears. "Don't you remember when we were little, how we liked the same games and played with the same dolls? We used to gather flowers to make crowns; we ate hazelnuts together. . . ."

"Even so, you are different. What about your wine that Christians aren't allowed to touch? That, by the way, is very upsetting for us. And your synagogue where you go every Saturday instead of going to church on Sundays? What do you do in your synagogue anyway? Everyone wonders. And even you yourself are different. You know how to read and write . . . and there are your ointments and potions. . . ."

Hardly able to speak, Elvina murmurs, "But your sister just asked me to give her some medicine for you!"

"I like your infusions and they do me good, but I'm not telling you anything new when I say that people around here whisper about your family. They say that all of you know a little too much about witchcraft."

Elvina is speechless. She wants to run away but has no idea how to go about it. She tries to extricate herself from Jeanne's grasp, but Jeanne is stronger than she is. Jeanne keeps her grip on Elvina, and now that she has started nothing stops her. "How can you explain that your mother and grandmother managed to save Thibault's wife last year, when she was practically given up for dead?"

"They know the herbs," counters Elvina. "They know when to pick them and how to use them; that's all. Anyone can learn that."

"What about your grandfather, who cured our cows of that sickness that was killing them off? I was only a little girl, but I remember it. People talked about it."

"You're lying," replied Elvina furiously. "Everyone respects my grandfather."

"I'm only repeating what I've heard."

Elvina cannot think what to say. The fear rushes back and now it is worse than before because she wasn't expecting it, not here, not now. It has caught her off guard, and, verging on tears, she only manages to stammer, "I thought we were friends."

"We are friends, but there are things you can't deny."

Jeanne seems about to continue when Marguerite, deciding to play her role as elder sister, interrupts.

"That's enough!" She puts her arms around Elvina and wipes her eyes with a rough sleeve smelling of flour and milk. She kisses her and says soothingly, "Don't quarrel anymore. Look, Jeanne, you've made Elvina cry, when I am the one who invited her to come and visit us!"

Jeanne kisses her, too, and Marie, still sucking on a willow stem, comes shyly over from the corner where she has been watching. She takes Elvina by the hand and smiles.

"Don't cry," says Jeanne. "You know I didn't mean to upset you. Come and have some of my curd cheese; it will make you feel better."

Her friends give Elvina more hugs and kisses and persuade her to eat a big ladleful of curd cheese. Outside the sky is clearing. A faint ray of pale sunshine peeps into the room through the open door. It might have been a signal for happiness, but Elvina remains walled up by her fear. She hardly hears Marguerite's and Jeanne's voices with their kind words.

As Elvina is leaving, Jeanne says comfortingly, "In the springtime let's go gather strawberries, just as we used to. Would you like that?"

"Yes," Elvina replies. But her heart is no longer in it, for nothing is as it used to be.

XV

Aweek has already gone by since Miriam and Precious left the house. It has been two whole weeks since Elvina last slipped discreetly into the back of the younger boys' classroom, and tomorrow it will be the Sabbath once more!

As Elvina quietly opens the door to the school, she is thinking, *Mazal, Mazal, since you are the one who speaks up for me in heaven, please see to it that my Sabbath is calm and peaceful, even if the day of rest decreed by our Lord isn't as joyful as it should be.* The door is a heavy one of worm-eaten wood, and no matter how careful she is, it creaks on its rusty hinges. A narrow hallway leads from the door to the classroom, and that is where Elvina stops.

The first thing she notices is a thick pile of straw on the ground in the corner where she usually sits. It is here that she can listen to what goes on in the classroom, without anyone being able to reproach her for attending a class where a girl has no business being.

The straw smells fresh and sweet. Elvina smiles to herself, thinking that it cannot possibly have been lying here on the icy ground for the last two weeks! Could that mean that someone puts new straw down every few days? Just for the only person who ever comes to sit here . . . just for a certain Elvina?

Elvina remembers the first time she found a pile of straw in "her" corner. It was during the first cold spell of autumn. That morning she had found a shiny boar's tooth left on the straw as if by accident. No scribe could have dreamed of having a more beautiful boar's tooth to smooth his parchments! And that morning, like all the others, Obadiah had pretended not to notice Elvina's presence.

She sits down on the straw and takes a bone stylus and a wax tablet from her sleeve. Pulling her cape tightly around her, she casts her eyes over the classroom.

The room is poorly lit. On one side are two narrow windows, and on the other are two resin torches that produce more smoke than light. An open fire gives out a little heat, most of which escapes out of the windows along with some of the smoke. The smoke makes Elvina want to cough, but she has to stifle it. With luck

Samuel and Yom Tov won't see her! They are sitting in the front row, with their backs to her. This is their last year in the younger boys' school. Elvina is glad to think that next year she will be able to come here without worrying about her brother and cousin and the embarrassing scenes they always make for her at home after school.

Obadiah ben Moyses, the master, is one of Solomon's pupils. He has chosen just the moment when Elvina closes the heavy door to turn his back on her and kneel down beside a row of five- or six-year-olds. As Solomon likes to remind his students, the scriptures say that a master should always place himself at his pupils' level and not talk down to them. Elvina can only see Obadiah's mane of black hair falling about his shoulders. *It is a mane*, thinks Elvina, *but a clean mane.* Obadiah's clothes, too, though patched and worn, have obviously just been washed. In the summer, keeping clean is easy. Everyone can go to the river to wash themselves and their clothes. But at this time of year, in winter, it's a different story! What is more, Obadiah lives in the school dormitory! Elvina wonders how he manages. She knows that he is the eldest son of a poor widow and that he has taken on teaching the little ones to make enough to live on while he studies, for he is proud and doesn't wish to owe anything to anyone. Elvina thinks of the previous master, Jacob ben Eliezer. He was thin, dirty, and always angry. His shrill voice rang out with the children's, especially when he was shouting, which was most of the time!

Although he is only nineteen, Obadiah has a deep voice, and he speaks with the even tones of a man who doesn't lose patience easily. "Now, read, and pronounce each syllable distinctly. Follow the text with your finger and show me each word as you say it."

The four little boys are reading a passage from Leviticus, the first book in the Bible to be read and learned. Obadiah has copied the passage onto two wax tablets. The four childish voices chant the Hebrew text in chorus, and Obadiah translates slowly:

"'All that which slithers on its belly, or moves on four feet or on a great number of feet, as do reptiles crawling along the ground, these thou shalt not eat, for these are unholy things.' Now it's your turn; repeat."

The four high voices repeat, "'All that which slithers on its belly . . .'"

"Good. Now tell me, which are the creatures that creep and crawl on the earth? We read it last week."

The boys all shout at once. "Mice, rats, tortoises!"

"Toads, centipedes!"

"Slugs, moles, hedgehogs, lizards!"

One of the children shrieks with laughter. "Who would want to eat a slug?"

"Our neighbors eat pigs!" retorts another.

"But we don't. For us it's forbidden . . ." says the third.

"Because we are the children of Israel!" pipes the fourth child.

"That's enough! Calm down." Obadiah taps a few of them on the head, but they are light taps, delivered by a friendly hand. Elvina knows he must be smiling, even though she can only see his back. In his left hand Obadiah holds a stick — what schoolmaster doesn't hold a stick or a whip? But he holds it as if it were a sprig of myrtle for a wedding dance. Elvina has never seen him use the stick to hit a pupil. Jacob ben Eliezer, on the other hand, would often whack the children smartly on the shoulder. Elvina remembers having left the classroom crying on more than one occasion, revolted by his unnecessary and useless brutality. Obadiah follows Solomon ben Isaac. Solomon teaches that one should always treat young pupils gently, so that they will learn to love studying.

Obadiah has risen to his feet. Of course Elvina doesn't look at him, but she sees him place his hands on the boys' heads. His large hands cover their heads completely.

"Now you will repeat this whole passage by yourselves until you can read it perfectly. Then you will learn it by heart. When we read the Torah, which is the divine Law, we must not stutter or stumble. Every word of the sacred language must be pronounced to perfection."

He pats their heads and then goes over to the other side of the room. This time he kneels down opposite Elvina, in front of Samuel and Yom Tov, who are in the front row. Obadiah speaks quietly, never raising his voice, but Elvina hears every word he says.

"It's your turn now. I'm listening." Obadiah gives the children his attention and they read. "'They brought before Moses the tabernacle and the tent and all the parts, staples, planks, pillars, and supports . . .'"

Half a dozen of them read the week's lesson together. Elvina can make out the voices of her brother and cousin, especially Yom Tov. She thinks to herself that nothing on earth will ever make her brother less conceited, even being captured by the Crusaders through his own stupidity.

"Let's explain the words." Obadiah begins. He often quotes Solomon, saying, "This is the way in which our master Solomon ben Isaac wishes us to interpret this verb; this is how he translates this difficult passage."

Elvina doesn't feel the long morning pass. She stays there in the warm little hallway, bent over her tablet, her head empty of everything except the words and the explanations, which she writes carefully on the wax with her stylus. She loves to hear her grandfather's explanations transmitted through the serious young voice of Obadiah.

She hears Obadiah continue, "Tomorrow, as you know, it is the Sabbath. After the morning service, our master Solomon ben Isaac will, as usual, give his commentary on these verses. He will explain that because Moses had not been able to do any work on the tabernacle, the Lord reserved for him the privilege of putting it up. Now, no one was strong enough to put it up because the planks were so heavy. Tomorrow Solomon ben Isaac will tell us how God ordered Moses, 'Get to work, and it will seem as if you had built it yourself.'"

Yom Tov sits bolt upright, almost standing in his seat. He gesticulates madly, his hair wild and his cape slipping halfway off his shoulders. He yells out proudly, "The tabernacle arose by itself! My grandfather already told us about it at home!"

"Very good. Sit down," says Obadiah with his eyes

directed straight at Yom Tov. But for an instant his gaze shifts from the unbearable younger brother to the back of the class, where the elder sister is crouching out in the hallway. Only for an instant, but an instant too long! The boy in the back row is yawning and dozing, his head buried deep inside his hood. But from under his hood he sees his master's gaze. This wakes him up, and he turns around. Spying Elvina, he points her out to his neighbor. The neighbor taps the shoulder of the boy in front of him. From nudge to nudge the word goes around. It doesn't take long, for it doesn't have far to travel. In less than one minute, the news is whispered into Yom Tov's ear.

Elvina is still bending over her tablet as if nothing else exists in the world, but she does not need eyes to know that her brother and cousin are livid with anger. She can almost hear the complaints that they will repeat later that evening to anyone who cares to listen. "Elvina will make us die of shame," they will say. "Everyone laughs at us. No one else's sister studies like a boy, let alone comes to school for everyone to see!"

Elvina also knows that Solomon ben Isaac will silence them.

From the corner of her eye, Elvina sees Obadiah brandishing his stick high above the boys' heads, which are once more bent earnestly over the parchments and tablets. Even the torches tremble at the sound of Obadiah's voice, and they smoke even more than before. "Read. Read loudly and clearly, and read properly; concentrate. You shouldn't think of anything else when you are reading the holy text."

Elvina pulls her hood over her face and smiles. She thinks that when Moses spoke to the Hebrews in the desert, his deep voice must have made them bow their heads in exactly the same way.

XVI

Mazal, O Mazal, where are you hiding? Have you given up looking after me? Or were you the one who inspired me this afternoon? What I did was so unexpected and so strange that even I don't recognize myself. Who can I confide in, if not you? That's why I've been silently talking to you ever since I started preparing the table for the Sabbath.

Zipporah and I swept everything clean, so that not the slightest crumb was left. We put away all the dishes and pots, and I filled the lamp with oil. In my mother's absence, I am the mistress of the house. When the time is right, I will light the Sabbath lamp, and I will bless the Lord, who commands us to light it. I have put out clean clothes for Samuel and Yom Tov. The sweet smell of meat gently stewing with spices and vegetables gradually fills the house. All is well, and the Sabbath will be welcomed in as it should be.

But despite all this, my dear Mazal, I have to admit that my heart and mind are not in it. I keep seeing myself in the street on the way home from school. I had just seen our neighbor Simonet's cart go by. It was piled high with supplies for the Crusaders. Simonet was leading the horse, and as he passed, he cried out to me, "It's my turn to do the dirty work today! How long is this going to go on?"

Just as I was turning onto the narrow street that leads home, the church bell pealed out midday. I told myself that I had no time to lose, because in winter the day is soon over. The bell stopped ringing, and there was a moment of silence as a sunbeam glinted against the street. Then I heard a bird's cry, followed by a long whistle. At first I thought it was another bird, but the sound seemed to be coming from the ground. The street was deserted. I looked around for the beggar near the bottom of the walls and even in the gutter, but I didn't see him. Then the whistling stopped.

Between two of the houses, there is a space, a kind of burrow, where abandoned dogs sometimes find shelter. I wondered if the beggar had gone in there, feeling too sick to crawl around the neighborhood as he had been doing for so long. Perhaps he had dragged himself into that hole to die. I felt so sorry for him that I drew closer. Mazal, what kind of trick were you playing on me? You know perfectly well who I found in the dog hole with his face and hair covered in mud! It was the young wounded Crusader, the one they call Gauthier! He really scared me! And it was even worse when he stretched out his arm, caught me by the sleeve, and pulled me toward him. I stumbled, slipped, and then there we were, face-to-face inside that horrible little space!

He was still holding on to my sleeve, and he smiled at me. "You don't need to be frightened," he said. "But if you stay out in the street they'll see you, and they'll wonder who you are talking to. Then they'll find me."

"Are you hiding? Are you sick?" I asked, trying not to let my fear show.

"I'm hiding, but I'm no longer sick," he replied. "Thanks to you, my leg is nearly healed. That's why, when I saw you pass by all by yourself, I whistled. You are the only one who can help me."

"Me? Help you? You must be joking! Let me go on my way."

"Please, just listen. You know I have to leave for the Crusade."

I nodded.

"Well, I'd rather die right now than go there. I hate fighting. It's not that I'm a coward; believe me, I'm not afraid of anything. But ever since I was a child, the only thing I have ever wanted to do was study. I can stay hidden in this hole for weeks. It's big enough. Look, I can even stretch out and lie down. If I stay here until Peter the Hermit gives the signal to leave, they'll give up looking for me. There's a monastery I can go to where the monks will take me in and let me study."

Mazal, O Mazal, there I was, in a hole, all alone, face-to-face with someone who is neither Tova nor Muriel nor even Jeanne or Marguerite, but a boy whose eyes made me think of clear, fresh water. And this boy had a kind voice. He expressed himself gently, and his hand rested on my arm.

"You are the only one who can help me," he repeated. "All I ask is that you bring me food and drink."

Although they are always saying I talk too much, for once I found myself speechless. Then the boy continued. "Think about it. I could help you, too."

I stammered, "How could *you* help *me*?"

"If you or your family are in any danger, I will warn you. Then you will be able to defend yourselves. You can save your people — just like Queen Esther."

Mazal, can you imagine how amazed I was to hear this? And then the boy began to laugh!

"Don't sit there with your mouth open; you'll get dirt in it! Did you think you were dealing with an ignorant peasant? An illiterate farm boy? Well, now you know! I've read the Bible, I know Latin, and that's just the beginning. I told you I'd rather die than have to give up studying. I didn't make this decision lightly, for it is a noble deed to go and recapture our Lord's tomb."

He was no longer laughing, and I found my tongue. "If you are holed up in here, how will you know what the Crusaders are doing?"

"My elder brother knows where I am. He loves weapons and acts of bravery and dreams of going to battle. He'd fight anyone. But he loves me and will not betray me."

"Can't your brother bring you food?" I asked.

"He would have to steal it, and if he came here every day my uncles would soon get suspicious. But you live right nearby, and no one would ever suspect you." Gauthier squeezed my arm tightly. "Please say you agree. I promise you will be informed of every plan Peter the Hermit dreams up against the Jews."

Mazal, where were you at that moment while I was telling myself that, thanks to me, my father would be warned in time? It's true that the small familiar voice inside me instantly whispered, "Don't get mixed up in men's affairs, girl. Your father and grandfather don't need you to tell them what to do."

Was that by any chance your voice, Mazal? If it was, then you did everything you could, and I shouldn't blame you! But I didn't take heed of that little voice; I only retorted, "Think of Queen Esther —"

The little voice rudely interrupted me, saying, "Have you gone crazy? Who do you think you are to compare yourself to Queen Esther! Anyway, she was only obeying the wishes of her Uncle Mordecai, whereas you, just for a change, are getting yourself involved in . . . goodness knows what!"

Gauthier had finally let go of my arm, but he was still feeling about my sleeve. "What do you have in there?" he asked when he came across the tablets. "You don't know how to write, do you?" he asked in astonishment.

"I can read *and* write," I replied coolly, bringing out

my tablets to show him, pleased with the opportunity to gain a little time.

"Did you write this?" he asked.

I nodded.

"What kind of writing is it?" he asked again.

"It's our holy language, which the Almighty gave to my people. He used it to dictate his Law to Moses, who is our teacher."

"I have read the Bible in Latin," Gauthier said.

"But Latin is just a translation. It's not a holy language. It's just an ordinary language like the one we are speaking right now."

Now it was Gauthier's turn to be speechless. He had probably never heard a girl talk this way. "And I can tell you something else," I continued. "Your Jesus spoke our holy language. All Jews know that!"

"I know it, too. The monks taught me." He frowned, then continued with his request. "Please say you'll help me. Bring me food in your sleeves. No one will notice. Women are always hiding things in their sleeves; that's what those wide sleeves are for. When I was little, I would hunt around in my mother's sleeves, and I always found some treat she'd kept for me. She was a good and gentle woman. If she were still alive, I know she would have taken my side against my uncles, and she would have convinced them to let me study. Then I wouldn't be holed up in here like a dog." His voice had started to quiver. "Do you remember how dark it was last night? There was just a tiny crescent of a moon!"

At this, his eyes filled with tears that spilled down his cheeks, mingling with the dust. He wiped them with his hands, but his hands were dirty with earth and streaked mud all over his face. Amid all this filth, I saw only his clear eyes brimming with tears. In that hole, all I could see was a boy my age, a lonely boy who missed his mother. I thought of my mother in Ramerupt, and I started crying, too. Then I promised Gauthier that I would bring him something to eat. "You won't tell on me, will you?" he whispered. He had stopped crying; his eyes were staring into mine, and I was staring back.

"What do you take me for?"

"You are a girl, and girls talk."

"I'm not like the others," I said. "I'll show you that a girl can hold her tongue. But don't *you* forget your promise."

Mazal, that's why I'm in such a hurry now. In a few minutes, I'm going to pretend that I have to feed my uncle's ewe and that I have one last errand to run. I'll rush off with my sleeves stuffed full of bread and cheese — and I'll put in an onion, too, because onions keep your strength up. I'm also taking some vials of water; a jug would look too obvious.

Oh, Mazal, please make sure I don't run into a soul!

XVII

"Armimas, rmimas, mimas, imas, mas, as . . ."

The girls and women dance in a circle and sing. Muriel and Bella, Naomi and Rachel, and their two identical mothers are all there, as well as the wife and daughters of Nathan ben Simon, the tanner, and the apothecary's wife, and of course Elvina and other neighborhood women. The street echoes with their laughter. They are all chanting: "Armimas, rmimas . . ." and some of them even think they can see the wicked demon whose specialty is attacking students to make them forget everything they learn. Yes, there he goes; they can just see him, so ugly and clumsy and crestfallen, now. . . . That's him, shrinking and shrinking as they shorten his name, because without a name he cannot exist. Then they laugh at his defeat, all the while holding hands and dancing around Judah ben Nathan who has just brought little Toby home from his first day at school. Judah is holding little Toby aloft. Toby is the only son of Nathan ben Simon, born after several girls.

Today is Toby's fourth birthday. His father has decided to educate his son better than he himself was educated or, indeed, his father and grandfather before him, tanners one and all. Nathan ben Simon has begged Judah ben Nathan to do him the immense honor of taking Toby, his only son among all those girls, for his first day at the school.

And so this morning Judah ben Nathan came to pick up little Toby. He lifted him high in his arms, wrapped him in a prayer shawl, and then hid him under his coat. This was to keep him from being seen by any demon who might think of harming him on this day when he was to be introduced to the holy letters. The *mazzikim* have no shadows, but they do have bodies, eyes, and ears, and they are always on the lookout for young, vulnerable prey.

As he was wrapping the child in his prayer shawl, Judah proclaimed, "Toby, son of Nathan, today you represent the children of Israel who left Egypt in order to receive the tablets of the Law at the foot of Mount Sinai."

Nathan the tanner and his wife were weeping with pride and joy. Elvina's eyes welled up with tears as she watched. She was moved to see the parents' respect and gratitude toward Judah.

"Hide his face well," someone said. "The boy must not come within sight of any dogs, nor must he look at one, for that would be a bad omen."

"Shhh!" said Nathan's wife. "Do you think you have to tell Judah ben Nathan what to do?"

She glanced anxiously at Judah, but he was laughing. "Don't worry," he said. "He will see no dogs, and no dog will see him, for it is written: 'Against the sons of Israel, no dog shall point his tongue.'"

It had been a long time since Elvina had seen her father in such a good mood. Muriel and Bella gave Nathan ben Simon three little honey cakes they had baked especially for the occasion, as well as an apple and an egg, for a child who is about to go to school must have something to eat. They also gave him a small pot of honey. Then Judah, still carrying Toby, set off toward the school, followed by Nathan ben Simon and his brother, Joseph ben Simon, Muriel's father.

Then the girls and women sat down to wait for the men's return. The winter was nearly over, and they dragged benches and stools out into the street, so as to sit comfortably, spinning and chatting in the warm sunshine.

Toby's sisters were waiting for him at the corner of the street. No way were they going to miss the future schoolboy's return from his initiation!

Rachel and Naomi sat on either side of Elvina. They seemed troubled and gloomy, and for once they were silent. Rachel was staring obstinately at her feet and swinging them to and fro. Naomi was frowning. Their spindles and staffs lay abandoned on a bench.

Naomi spoke first. "They're making him lick the sacred letters, aren't they, Elvina?"

"Yes," Elvina began. "First they give him the honey cakes, then the apple and the egg —"

"Yes, yes," they interrupted. "We know that already, but what happens next?"

"Then Obadiah gives him a wax tablet with the sacred letters on it. He spells them for Toby, one by one, pointing them out with his finger."

"And then?"

"Then Obadiah spreads honey on all the letters, and Toby licks it off so that he will taste the sweetness of the Torah. Then they all gather around Toby and congratulate him and dance around him. Of course,

Obadiah's pupils love this extra break time, and they try to make it last as long as possible."

Without doing it on purpose, at least not absolutely on purpose, Elvina had mentioned Obadiah's name no fewer than three times. Surely the twins were going to jump at the chance to tease her mercilessly! Elvina prepared herself for the onslaught, but none came. There was silence. It was as if the twins had become not only mute, but deaf as well. Rachel continued rocking back and forth on the bench, swinging her feet as high as she could, and Naomi continued to frown and stare into space.

"And what about us?" asked Rachel, finally. "Why don't *we* get all that? Why don't they let *us* lick the sacred letters? They don't even show them to us. Why, Elvina? Why?" She was on the verge of tears.

Before Elvina had time to answer, Bella, who had been following the conversation from her footstool, answered for her. "What a stupid question! It's because you're girls, and what is normal for boys isn't normal for girls. That's all there is to it."

Naomi glared at her elder sister as if she wanted to hit her. "We all know that the only thing that interests you is how to please your future husband."

"And what's wrong with that?"

There was another long silence between the girls as the spinning women gossiped away around them, explaining to everyone who passed why the shops of Nathan the tanner and Joseph the furrier were closed. The passersby congratulated Toby's mother.

Then, at the very same moment, the twins whispered to Elvina, one in each ear so nobody else could hear. "Show us the letters! Teach us to read!" they begged. They moved closer, and once they had started, there was no stopping them. They threw their arms around Elvina, stroked her hair, and competed with each other to see who could hug her the hardest. "Please, Elvina!" they begged.

"Ouch, you're suffocating me!" Their warm mouths remained glued to her ears.

"Say you will, Elvina; say you will teach us!" they whispered over and over.

Elvina closed her eyes, and a smile crept across her lips.

"Well?" asked the twins.

"Well, Solomon ben Isaac, my grandfather, says that there is nothing in our Law that forbids educating girls."

"Are you saying yes?" they asked, looking at Elvina expectantly.

"Yes!"

The twins were overjoyed. "Can we begin today?" they urged.

"Yes, we'll begin today," replied Elvina.

The three girls jumped down from their bench and began to dance with joy. They were dancing wildly and in full view of everyone.

The twins' mother dropped her spinning in surprise and scolded, "What's gotten into you girls?"

But just then, Toby's sisters shouted, "Here they come!"

All the women rushed to meet Judah ben Nathan, who still carried Toby in his arms, hidden in the folds of his coat. At the sound of his mother's and sisters' voices, the boy peeked out, his face still smeared with honey.

Now little Toby, thrilled that he is the center of attention, smiles down at the women. They all dance around him, but none of them dance as joyfully as Naomi, Rachel, and Elvina. They jump higher and shout louder than any of the others, "Armimas, rmimas, mimas . . ." to upset the wicked Armimas, demon of stupidity and forgetfulness, and shrink him out of existence, so that he will never ever dare to harm Toby . . . or Naomi or Rachel!

My dear Mazal, what shall I do? Once again I have acted without thinking. I hate this secret that keeps me awake at night. I am not Esther, acting under the guidance of Mordecai. I am only a girl who has done something terribly stupid. . . . Perhaps I have even sinned! It's been a week now, and soon the Sabbath will return.

This morning, with all the singing and dancing, I forgot. For a whole morning I forgot about Gauthier, while he, poor thing, was alone in his hole, crying and scratching his earth-covered skin.

Later on, I remembered him and my promise. I ran to take him some bread and cheese, but I threw them in at him without stopping, just as if I had been throwing food at a dog. I'm ashamed that I did that, but I'm also ashamed of my terrible secret.

This morning, my father, Judah ben Nathan, was laughing while he lifted Toby into the air. If he only knew! If he only knew that his daughter was hiding a Crusader!

When I got home, Solomon ben Isaac was pleased. A messenger had come from Ramerupt to say that my Aunt Yochebed had a baby girl, whom she has called

Hannah. My Uncle Meir will bring back my grandmother tomorrow, before the Sabbath, and my mother will return next week.

But as for me, Mazal, instead of being glad, I thought, *How on earth can I keep all this from my grandmother's sharp eyes? How will I manage to prevent her from noticing anything?*

And then there's my grandfather. My whole life I have confided in him, but now I hardly dare look him in the face.

I made a promise, and that surely must mean something. If I break it, Gauthier will be right to despise me. He will say that girls are not to be counted on after all. On the other hand, he hasn't told me a thing about the Crusaders' plans. Do you think, by any chance, he is deceiving me?

Mazal, Mazal, what shall I do?

XVIII

"Don't run away; keep me company, not like last time. My tongue is numb and hardly remembers how to speak. Soon I won't be able to utter a single word. I can't keep on talking to myself like a babbling old woman!"

Huddled down in the burrow, Gauthier tries to laugh, but his eyes give him away. They are red, and his eyelids are irritated and swollen. He grabs Elvina's sleeve as she is about to offer him a piece of bread, and he doesn't let go.

"Don't be afraid!" he says as he draws her toward him. "Last night I cleaned out my little home as well as the best housewife could. And *I* am clean, too. I've washed myself." Gauthier smiles; then he continues, "The moon will soon be full, and the nights are not so dark. While the town was asleep, I walked to the river. I saw that spring had arrived; the apple trees were in bloom, and the moonlight shone through the flowers, making the blossoms look even whiter. The night air was warm, and the water was cold but not icy."

As he speaks, a dreamy look comes into his eyes. "You can't imagine how good it felt to duck my head under the water. I drowned all the fleas that were tormenting me! I lay down on the riverbank where it is on the same level as the water. You must know the place, because I'm sure the women go there to do their washing. I did my washing, too. Then I lay there on my back looking up at the clouds, racing across the sky, playing with the moon. Let me tell you, those apple trees smelled wonderful." He sniffs the air as if to bring back their scent. "Imagine that, after so many days and nights in this hole!"

Gauthier talks as a thirsty man drinks, without stopping to draw breath. Elvina listens to him gladly, thinking of the ballads her Aunt Rachel used to read to her in secret by candlelight. It is true, Gauthier speaks like a poet. . . .

"But I was hungry," he begins again. "Why didn't you come last night? Did you forget me?"

"Last night was the Sabbath. Just before *Havdalah* I went to see my friend Tova and her baby. After Havdalah, I couldn't go out again, and night had fallen.

Then my grandmother came home, and she constantly watches me."

"What is Havdalah?" asks Gauthier.

"It's the prayer we say when the Sabbath ends and everyday life returns. We watch for three stars to come out in the sky, then we light the fire and the lamps again, and we bless the light. We burn spices so that their perfume spreads through the whole house and gets rid of the bad smells that Satan sends us."

"Satan sends you bad smells?" he asks.

"Yes, because he wants to take his revenge for all the evil he has not been able to do during the Sabbath! But look here, I've brought you a real feast; a big piece of meat that I managed to hide while no one was looking, two honey cakes, and some nuts. I'm sorry, but I couldn't bring you any gravy for the meat!"

Elvina is squatting down in the hole. She watches Gauthier as he wolfs down the bread and meat, then the cakes, and finally the nuts, which he cracks open with his teeth. She thinks about how brave he is and how her brother and cousin, with their easy and sheltered existence, would never be able to bear what this boy with the light blue eyes is enduring.

Gauthier wipes his mouth and starts talking again. "Last night I saw my mother in a dream. She gave me fruit, not just ordinary apples but juicy golden pears. I think that means she's in heaven and that she's watching over me."

Elvina agrees wholeheartedly, "Yes, I'm sure that is what it means."

But Gauthier is not listening to her. He is already talking about something else. "I know everyone who passes by my hole, at least by sight. There are schoolboys for example. I can guess which one is your brother; he looks like you. He's thin and dark, and he always walks with a red-haired boy who also looks like you."

"That's my cousin Samuel."

"They don't know how lucky they are, all those Jewish boys who spend their days studying as if it were the most natural thing in the world. What wouldn't I give to be in their place! But I can't turn myself into a Jew!"

"Don't Christian boys study?"

"Only if their parents want them to become priests. In my family they expect a boy to become a warrior, not a cleric. When my mother was alive, I was able to study with the monks, but the very day after she died my uncles said that I was quite educated enough and that it was time I learned to handle a sword. They wouldn't let me return to the monks."

Gauthier pushes his hair back with an impatient gesture. "But I want to study. You see why you absolutely must continue to help me. It's my only chance. Now tell me what goes on in this town, Troyes, that you know so well and I not at all."

Elvina shakes her head. "I don't know what goes on in Troyes, but I can tell you about the Sabbath."

"Go on then; tell me."

Elvina takes her mind back to the contented hours she has just spent with her family. "We had the Sabbath meal at my grandfather's, Solomon ben Isaac's. My grandmother had prepared everything. It was almost like before."

"Before what?"

"Before you . . . well, you know . . . I mean before Peter the Hermit arrived."

"I understand." He nods. "Go on."

"Around the table, only my mother, Miriam, was missing. There were several of my grandfather's students and two travelers whom my grandfather invited because they were passing through Troyes. One of them has been as far as the land of Israel and even farther — all the way to Baghdad. He has seen flying camels, which are also called dromedaries. He has seen elephants and he told us how they eat."

Gauthier looks puzzled; then Elvina explains, "An elephant is a huge gray animal with a long nose that it uses to reach out for its food and put it into its mouth. Everything we do with our hands, the elephant does with its long nose. An elephant is so strong, it can carry twelve armed warriors! The other merchant had nothing exciting to tell us, but he has his own personal clock that he wears attached to his belt."

"He has a clock of his own?" Gauthier's blue eyes are wide with surprise.

"Yes. It's a long silver tablet with gold edges, and it has holes in it. The names of the months are carved in pairs in a certain order. You hold the silver tablet by a chain and put a little silver peg into one of the holes, depending on the month it is, and then the peg's shadow falls on signs, which mark the hours. So the traveler can know what time it is whenever he likes, in the forest or at sea. All he needs is a ray of sunlight, as the merchant said. It really is magnificent!"

Elvina remembers the astonishment in Solomon ben Isaac's eyes. He looked even more amazed than the boys! First he weighed the clock in his hands and admired its lightness, and then he went over to the window so that the light shone on the dial. He called everyone over to come and read the time, not only the family but also his pupils and even the servants.

"And what did you talk about during the meal?" Gauthier asks.

"My grandfather explained some points in the week's readings and told us how the Lord loved Moses, who is our teacher. I was helping my grandmother to serve, but not a word of what was being said escaped me. Sabbath conversations are always so interesting."

She thinks of Obadiah and his deep gentle voice. She can hear his words from the end of the table where she sits when she isn't serving. He always asks Solomon such intelligent questions and listens to the answers with such respectful attention.

She thinks again of the way Obadiah raised his eyes to her and how he nodded his head in thanks when she refilled his glass and later when she handed him a honey cake.

Obadiah's beard is thick and black like a grown man's, but even when he makes fun of someone, as he does occasionally, he never looks arrogant.

Elvina doesn't mention any of this to Gauthier, but the memory of Obadiah's smile must have lit up her face fleetingly, for Gauthier immediately says, "There was someone there whom you have not told me about."

Elvina shakes her head. She feels herself blushing and hates herself for it. She blushes even more, shakes her head again, and finally gives a little laugh. "No, there was no one else."

Elvina tells herself that she is being just as ridiculous as Bella, but Gauthier doesn't make fun of her. "It's only natural. You're a pretty girl, and I'm sure your parents will have no trouble finding you a husband."

"Maybe," says Elvina; then she changes the subject. "Has your brother come to you? Did he say anything?"

"Yes, but he only stayed a couple of minutes," replies Gauthier. "He was worried they might notice his absence. He told me that Peter the Hermit will soon give the order for us to leave. He wants to head for Germany."

At this, Elvina remembers what her grandfather has told her. "Several men," she says, "including my father, are supposed to be taking letters to this famous Peter the Hermit one day soon. The letters are for our brothers in Germany, asking them to give Peter and his men the provisions they need in return for the safety of our people and their property."

"You'll see, it'll turn out all right in the end." Gauthier smiles.

Elvina, feeling reassured, continues. "If only your

troops could leave on the day of Purim, without harming us or burning our houses! That would be a really special Purim for the Jews of Troyes. Tomorrow is the fast of Esther. I am going to fast for the first time in my life, just like Esther fasted before going to find her husband, King Ahasuerus."

"If you were Esther, I would be Ahasuerus and you would have to marry me. All I'm asking for is a bit of bread and water, so you get off lightly! Don't look so horrified! My eyes are itching; do you know what that means?"

Elvina takes a closer look at Gauthier and answers him earnestly. "It means that they have got more dust and earth in them than they can bear, poor things. Tomorrow even my fast won't stop me from bringing you a very good ointment. It's made from pigeon droppings. In two days, your eyes will be better."

Gauthier laughs. "Thank you," he says. "Bring me your ointment, but you should know what it means to have itching eyes. It's the sign that soon these very eyes will be reading again, reading all the books they haven't yet read! It means I'll soon be studying again! That's what it means!"

XIX

The market is in full swing this eve of Purim. People are fasting, but this doesn't stop them from preparing the festivities for the evening and the following day. Then there are the presents: presents for friends and neighbors and also for the poor, for they, too, are supposed to receive gifts. The cake seller has really outdone herself, with mountains of honey cakes and cakes made with figs and nuts piled up on her trestle for clients who have no oven or do not want to make their own sweets. The spice merchant is also as busy as can be. Cinnamon, ginger, and saffron are in great demand.

Elvina and the twins have just run into the old beggar, who drags himself toward Elvina. His tongue lolls out and he dribbles onto his beard.

"My little lady, will you have anything to give me

tomorrow? You see, today I am fasting like all the other children of Israel."

"Try to come to our house tomorrow," replies Elvina. "You will eat and drink like a king, and my father will give you some money."

The old man laughs. "But if I stay in your courtyard no one will see me, so I'll get fewer presents and less money!"

"Do as you like. I'll find you."

Naomi and Rachel impatiently fidget and tug at Elvina's coat. "This old man is not as stupid as he pretends to be, and anyway, we want to read. Come on!"

"But where shall we hide? Elvina, do you have any ideas?" asks Naomi.

"We can go down the street, behind Dieulesault the blacksmith's cart," Elvina suggests. "Nobody will think of looking for us behind scythes and spare parts for plows! And the blacksmith's clients are all men. They won't be interested in what three little girls are doing bent over a tablet. And we'll be far from the tempting smell of those cakes! Don't forget that today I'm fasting!"

"So are Muriel and Bella," says Naomi.

"Our turn will come in two years," adds her sister.

"But we've hardly eaten anything today, have we, Naomi?"

"No, we just wanted to get away from the house! Muriel gave us hundreds of dried beans and lentils to sort for tomorrow's meal. We hid them in a jug and ran off. We can sort them very quickly later."

Dieulesault stares at the three girls. His eyes are as red as the smoldering coals he bends over all day long. He gestures the girls toward a clean, flat stone where they can sit down.

"The granddaughter of our master Solomon ben Isaac is welcome behind my stall. Whatever you are up to, it can't be anything bad, and anyway, it's none of my business."

Dieulesault has powerful shoulders, huge arms, and a voice that booms louder than the bellows of his forge.

This morning he has left his cave filled with dancing red shadows reflecting the forge fire. He has taken off his thick leather apron, and he has come to the market to display the tools he has for sale. It will soon be time for the men to start working the land, turning the earth, plowing the furrows. Axes, scythes, spades, and hoes are piled up on his cart, as well as two plowshares and a rake for breaking up clods of earth and leveling out the ground for the seed.

If Dieulesault were listening, he might hear the words drifting over from where the girls are sitting.

"Bereshit bara Elohim . . ."

Hunched over the wax tablet, where Elvina has copied out the first few verses of the Bible, their heads stuck one against the other, Naomi and Rachel painstakingly make out each syllable. Their eyebrows furrow with effort, their mouths pronounce every word of the Hebrew text with care and reverence. They read together as if they had but one voice between them. At the end of the verse, both heads look up together. They are breathless, as if they'd been running, but proud, as if they had just won a battle.

Elvina claps her hands, exclaiming, "What good students you are! I'm proud of you both!"

"We are studying as hard as we can," say the twins. "Whenever we have a minute to ourselves, we take out the tablet where you have written the letters for us, and we review them."

Elvina smiles. "And today you are reading the sacred text. It's a big day for you both, and for me, too!"

Naomi looks up anxiously at the overcast sky. "I hope it's not going to rain, at least not yet."

"Let's not waste time," says Elvina. "Follow my finger; we're going to translate, word by word. 'In the beginning, God created the heavens and the earth. Now the earth was '*tohu* and *bohu*' —"

"What's '*tohu*'?" asks Naomi.

"And what's '*bohu*'?" echoes her sister.

Elvina puts on the same tone of voice she has often heard Obadiah use. "'*Tohu*' means unformed. But Solomon ben Isaac interprets it with the words *astonishment* and *amazement*. As for '*bohu*,' which means void, he says *emptiness* and *solitude*. Now, read it again, again, and again until you can do it perfectly. A sacred text must be read without stumbling or hesitation."

Sometimes Dieulesault's voice drowns out the girls'. "Who wants nails? Who needs hammers?" Then more quietly, "I have knives and daggers that I made this winter. Crusaders came looking for them and I swore that I didn't have any!"

But Elvina and her pupils don't let themselves get distracted. "Read the second verse again, and repeat the translation. Show me word for word as you translate."

"'. . . And the spirit of God moved upon the surface of the waters,'" they read.

"Would you like to know how my grandfather interprets that?"

"Yes, tell us."

"He explains that the throne of divine glory was standing in space, hovering over the face of the waters."

"The throne hovered in the air?" Naomi asks in wonder.

"Like a dove that hovers over its nest," says Elvina.

"What dove? What are you talking about?" Another voice joins in their conversation.

None of the three girls had noticed Matriona running toward them. Matriona is Dieulesault's daughter. She is ten, like the twins. She is friendly with them and sometimes gives them pins that her father has given her. "What are you doing? What are you hiding?" she begins, but right away, without waiting for a reply, she continues. "Over there is a merchant with a monkey. I've never seen anything so funny in my life! He has tiny eyes and odd little hands, and when you give him an apple he eats it making the funniest faces! Why are you looking at me like that? Don't you believe me? Come and see."

"Leave us alone with your monkey," Rachel retorts. "Do you think we have never seen a monkey before? Anyway, he's not worth seeing. We are busy reading!"

"Hush!" Naomi claps her hand over her sister's

mouth and whispers furiously. "If they find out, they'll stop us! Then we'll never know how to read properly!"

With her other hand Naomi pushes Matriona away. "Don't worry about us; go back and admire your monkey."

"Whatever you like," replies Matriona, "but I don't understand you at all!"

Rachel has turned red and is verging on tears. "I'm so sorry! I'll never mention it again. I promise."

A drop of rain falls onto the wax tablet. Elvina thinks of Gauthier in his hole. He is waiting for her. She would like to go there and not find him. She would like to find the hole empty. She feels tired. She has prepared the ointment for his eyes, and before the first stars come out she will have to bring him enough food to last a whole day, because tomorrow during the festivities she will not be able to take him anything. And even today, how is she supposed to bring him food without being noticed? Today all the Jews are fasting. Yes, she really is tired of this particular secret!

"It's raining," she says. "Soon the street will be empty, and they'll come looking for us."

"Listen to us read just one more time," insist the twins.

They read again, and, when they get to the end of the three verses, they start over. They can't stop reading, and they can't help smiling as they read, chanting the sentences a little, as they have heard the men do in the synagogue. The raindrops fall harder and harder on the tablet. They wipe it dry with their fingertips, lightly, so as not to rub out the precious letters, the words of the sacred text.

"We are reading; we are no longer ignorant; we are students, your students. . . ."

Elvina hugs them. "You are excellent students. Tomorrow, in honor of Purim, not only will I give you sweets like Muriel and Bella, but I'm also going to give each of you a secret present: your very own brand-new wax tablet with a bone stylus. Soon you will know how to write! But remember, you must never write during the Sabbath, because that is the day of rest. Today I'll leave this tablet with you. Learn the three verses by heart. Tomorrow you'll learn three more."

It's raining in earnest now. The girls put up their hoods and Naomi hides the tablet up her sleeve. Then she takes it out again.

"Just write our names; write 'Naomi' and 'Rachel.' Please, Elvina."

Elvina takes her stylus and writes three Hebrew characters for Rachel, then four for Naomi.

"It's not fair; she has one more than me!" protests Rachel.

Elvina laughs and taps Rachel's head, which is hidden beneath her hood. "Haven't you ever noticed that words are not all the same length?"

When Elvina arrives home, she finds Solomon standing in front of his house. He welcomes his granddaughter with a smile. "Breathe in the smell of the rain and the wet earth. This is the soft first rain, which in the land of Israel is called *yoreh*. It prepares the earth for seeds to be sown. Breathe in deeply and listen, Elvina; listen to the sound of the rain on the roof. That pitter-patter is a sweeter and more peaceful sound than pure silence. It makes you forget that the countryside is full of wandering hordes who might, at any moment . . ." His voice trails off.

"Who might *what* at any moment?" Elvina asks. She holds her breath, waiting for her grandfather to answer.

"Nothing," he sighs. "At least I hope not. But we Jews always have to be ready to face catastrophe."

Elvina's heart leaps in her chest. Now it is thumping

madly. Far from being useful to her family, might she not, by helping a young Crusader, be guilty of causing the dreaded catastrophe?

"My granddaughter seems very worried."

Elvina swallows hard. Her hands are cold as ice. The words take shape in her head, and in spite of herself, they come tumbling out of her mouth. "There's something. . . ."

She is going to tell him. She is going to tell him that she took pity on the boy with blue eyes, that he promised to keep her informed of the Crusaders' plans. She is going to confess to her grandfather that she was stupid enough to take herself for Queen Esther. Solomon will tell her that it was wrong of her to have acted without thinking, but he will know what to do. He may even be able to help Gauthier. Poor Gauthier, deep in his hole, he must be soaked to his very bones.

In a low voice, now, she repeats, "There is something." She can almost hear Gauthier saying, "Girls talk." She shakes her head and asks, "Will we be able to have fun tomorrow?"

Solomon strokes her cheek. "Yes, but discreetly. We won't be singing and dancing in the courtyards and the streets. I think the men will not drink as much as usual, even though there is a tradition that says a man should be too drunk on Purim to know whether he should curse evil Haman or bless Mordecai!"

Solomon smiles and runs his fingers through his beard, looking at his granddaughter. "But I am sure it is not the thought of having fun more quietly than usual that is making my granddaughter look so pensive and worried! Is it because you miss your mother? The day after tomorrow, God willing, she'll be back. She's coming with a convoy of merchants."

A young man runs up, all out of breath, a piece of heavy sacking over his head to keep off the rain. "Master Solomon ben Isaac!" he cries. "There is a terrible quarrel about a piece of land. There's going to be trouble!"

Solomon puts his hand on Elvina's head. "You see, life goes on. People still buy and sell land and fight over it. Go join your grandmother; help her prepare for tomorrow. It's not good for you to stay alone. In a few hours both of you will come to the synagogue for the first reading of *The Book of Esther*."

Elvina watches her grandfather walk off at his regular pace. But his gray cloak, which wraps him up completely, seems larger than before, and under the hood his shoulders look slightly stooped.

Tonight it will be Purim.

XX

As soon as we finished reciting the evening prayer, the twins fell asleep. They were worn out and they snuggled up to each other and leaned against me. Their arms and legs — and even their hair — were intertwined. Next, Bella fell asleep and her regular breathing filled the room. Finally, Muriel bid me good night for the third time before drifting into slumber. She is still holding my hand in hers. How lucky they are to be sleeping.

Aunt Rachel, sweet Aunt Rachel, if only it were you in bed next to me! What a state your poor Gazelle is in! Trouble, fear, and remorse are spinning around in my head, while the terrible din, which blared out in the streets this evening, still fills my ears! How will I ever get to sleep?

Already Purim seems far away. It was a beautiful day, perfect for a holiday. The sky was blue and the sun warm; a light breeze pushed the clouds along like woolly lambs, and you could almost see the trees springing into leaf before your eyes.

Everyone was at the synagogue for the second reading of *The Book of Esther.* The women's section was packed. After all, Purim is a holiday that especially interests women and girls, because the main character in today's reading is a heroine! Rachel and Naomi made their way to where I was sitting, so that I could explain anything they didn't understand. The hall of the synagogue resounded with laughter and booing every time Haman's name was mentioned. That wicked Haman who had plotted to massacre the Jewish people.

The poor and the beggars were also happy, knowing they would be able to eat and drink their fill and get enough small change to live on for the next few months.

My grandfather invited his students to share the feast at his house. My grandmother and I worked hard along with the servants so that the table looked perfect for the occasion. We didn't skimp on the number of candles. Their flames remind us that Queen Esther restored the spark of life to the Jews. We placed bundles of straw around the table so that everyone would be able to sit down. As usual, every two guests would share one wooden platter and one goblet between them, but my father and grandfather each had his own magnificent silver platter.

As I was passing the plates around, I asked my father if he didn't think that Obadiah, being a schoolmaster, should get a plate and goblet to himself. Judah laughed and told me to do as I saw fit. He put his arm round Obadiah's shoulders and invited Obadiah to sit next to him. I noticed that Obadiah was blushing. When I served him some wine, he didn't look at me but nodded his head respectfully, as if I were not just a little girl! Yom Tov and Samuel were sitting on his left and made sure that their master's plate was never empty.

Everyone was in a good mood, masters and students, old and young alike. They discussed the meaning of *The Book of Esther* and also told jokes. Even Obadiah drank and laughed. He told a story, but I didn't get to hear it because just at that moment my grandmother, Precious, called me over. "All these boys are going to spend their time drinking and making a lot of noise," she said. "Why don't you go and spend the night at Muriel's? Zipporah will take you there."

While I was wrapping myself in my cloak, I glanced at my father. He glanced back at me, and

I couldn't help also seeing Obadiah out of the corner of my eye. He was looking at me. His cheeks were a little red and his dark eyes were shining, but it was not because he had drunk too much, like some of the other boys.

My grandmother doesn't miss a thing. She pulled my hood up over my head and ushered me toward the door. "Go on then, child; have a good time with your girlfriends. Get going before the first stars come out."

Solomon ben Isaac gave me another of his nice grandfatherly smiles, and then we left. My grandfather had told Zipporah to invite Muriel's father Joseph ben Simon, her uncle, Nathan ben Simon, and also the twins' father to join in the festivities at the house.

Zipporah and I walked quickly, because she was in a hurry to get back. Although the streets were empty, it didn't feel gloomy, since all the doors and shutters were open, and we could hear the singing and laughter of the neighborhood Jews celebrating the victory of Esther and Mordecai.

In a courtyard not far from ours, we caught sight of the old beggar who crawls around the streets. He was asleep, his head resting on a stone and his hand on his stomach, which for once must have been full. The courtyard echoed with his snoring.

I found my four friends, their identical mothers, their fathers, their uncle and aunt, and their cousins sitting around the table having fun. Little Toby had drunk some wine and was dozing in his mother's lap. When Zipporah announced my grandfather's invitation, the three men didn't wait to be asked twice. An invitation from Solomon ben Isaac! They left right away!

As for Zipporah, she left with both her sleeves full of goodies and was looking very happy.

Naomi and Rachel gave me some food, and Rachel whispered in my ear, "Be careful when you eat the lentils and beans. We sorted them so quickly that there is still quite a lot of sand in them!"

I drank some wine and we sang and laughed in the mild evening air. A cool breeze came in through the window with the milky light of the full moon. Several candles and two lamps stood on the table, and it was because of these, with their dancing flames, that at first we didn't notice anything. We didn't see the sky getting darker and darker.

We were too busy chatting and teasing Bella about her upcoming wedding. We were sure that by then the Crusaders would be gone and Bella's parents would be able to make a sumptuous feast at their house in the country. I told her I was sure that my grandfather,

Solomon ben Isaac, would dance to entertain the bride, because despite his gray beard, there is nothing he enjoys more than a dance! He arches his back and he twists and turns and follows the music better than some of the young people, waving his myrtle branch high in the air. But you should hear him complaining of his aches and pains the next day!

Everyone at the table was laughing, and none of us noticed that the light outside had faded and the sky had become black as pitch. Muriel's mother was the first to mention anxiously, "Didn't it get dark suddenly? Only moments ago it was light and there wasn't a cloud in the sky."

She walked over to the window, repeating how strange it was, because the sky was still cloudless. At that moment, we heard a noise coming from a neighboring street. It grew louder and louder like an approaching storm. Suddenly the twins' elder brother, Baruch, appeared out of the darkness, wrapped up from head to toe in his cloak and hood. Only his eyes were visible. He looked terrified.

"It's an eclipse of the moon!" he yelled. "There are at least a hundred men running through the streets brandishing weapons. They're firing arrows into the air and throwing lighted torches toward the moon, shouting, '*Vinceluna!*', the moon will conquer." As he spoke, he rushed over to the window and closed the shutter. His mother barred the door. We froze in fear, glued to our seats around the table and staring at one another in silence. We held hands to give ourselves courage.

I remembered an eclipse of the moon that had happened when I was little and my Aunt Rachel still lived with us. I remembered how she said to us then, "These people fire arrows into the sky because they think the moon is suffering, and they want to help her. The torches are meant to help light her up again. The men shout out to encourage her. It's nothing special; don't let it frighten you."

"They're only trying to help the moon," I said. "Let's not get excited."

Baruch was getting his breath back, downing great gulps of wine. His voice was hoarse. "I saw a priest among them," he said. "I'm sure of it. He was encouraging them, but I couldn't hear what he was saying because of their cries."

His mother was wringing her hands just like my grandmother, Precious, then said exactly what my grandmother was probably saying at that very moment:

"One of them just has to say that the moon's misfortune is the Jews' fault, and the others will follow him. . . ."

"They'll come and set fire to all the Jewish houses," continued Muriel's mother, who was even more upset.

"They're carrying torches!" added Baruch.

Again thinking of my Aunt Rachel, I said, "These Christians are our neighbors. They know us. They do not wish us any harm."

"Maybe. But what if the Crusaders join them?" asked Bella's mother. "The Crusaders don't know us and they *do* wish us harm!"

"And in our house there are only women and children!" cried Muriel's mother.

How I wished I were at home! I was sure that my father and grandfather would give a correct explanation for this frightening event and be able to make it less frightening. But returning home was out of the question. I might be brave, but I would never have dared set foot out in the streets. And in any case, they wouldn't have allowed me to leave.

We were all crying. Even little Toby was howling, though he didn't understand what was going on. Then came the sound of someone pounding on the door.

"Open up!" said a familiar voice.

We opened it a crack and saw the bloodred moon in the sky above the nearby houses. As soon as the three men had come in, we closed the door quickly. The two identical mothers cried and wailed, hanging on to their husbands, who were out of breath from running. How I longed to be at home!

Then I asked Nathan ben Simon, "What does my grandfather, Solomon ben Isaac, say?"

"He reminded us of the words of the prophet Jeremiah," Nathan ben Simon said. "'Fear not the signs of the heavens,' which, according to Solomon ben Isaac, means that those who carry out the will of the Holy One, blessed be He, should fear no punishment."

Joseph ben Simon leaned toward me and said kindly, "Solomon ben Isaac told me to reassure his granddaughter. And Judah ben Nathan told me to tell you that on no account should you try to go home. You must stay in the safety of our house until tomorrow. They both send you their blessing."

I burst into sobs. The more I thought of what my grandfather had said, the more desperate I felt. "Those who carry out the will of the Holy One!" I had hidden a Crusader! Muriel, Bella, Rachel, and Naomi were hugging me, trying to comfort me, but the more they tried, the harder I sobbed. They didn't understand why I was now the one trembling and crying. How could they ever have guessed?

Now that we are in bed, I dare not move, for fear of waking them. How could *they* help me? They have no answer to the question that is tormenting me. Everyone knows that an eclipse is a bad sign for the Jews, because it is the result of a sin. What nobody knows is that I, Elvina, have hidden, cared for, and comforted a Crusader. The Crusaders are the Jews' enemies. Might there not be some link between my actions and this warning from heaven? I am just a young and insignificant girl, and Gauthier, who is the same age as me, has never hurt a fly. Since the Almighty knows everything, He must also know that!

Where is my Mazal, who is supposed to guide and protect me? Is he speaking up for me in heaven now?

Around me there are only sleeping girls, a hooting owl, and the night with its silence. The night has cleared, thank God, and the moon has recovered her beautiful silvery face. I can hardly wait for the day to come, for this day should bring back my mother. But will she be able to return at a time like this? Who would venture out onto the roads?

XXI

un, girl, run; live up to your nickname, Gazelle. Run to the synagogue to warn your father. Run; don't stop! You can catch your breath later, thinks Elvina, as she runs toward the synagogue.

As soon as the day broke, Elvina had left Muriel's house and rushed to the school. She told herself that Obadiah's calm, deep voice explaining the lesson to the little ones would help clarify her troubled thoughts. Studying the sacred texts brings one closer to the Almighty. Surely He would inspire her with the right decision.

In the little hallway, not the slightest wisp of straw was to be seen. Elvina was about to sit down on the bare ground when Obadiah abruptly turned toward her and showed her the door with a single gesture of his hand. His lips were stern and his eyes cold. Elvina withdrew. Obadiah joined her in the courtyard. He was livid with anger.

"I am ashamed of you," he said. "You are hiding a Crusader. Someone saw you and told me about it last night. How could you do such a thing? You, the daughter and granddaughter of my esteemed masters? If you don't tell them immediately, I will. Don't you ever set foot in this school again!"

He didn't leave Elvina time to realize what was happening, let alone answer him. He turned on his heels and went back to his students. She thought she even heard him bolt the door behind him.

In the folds of her sleeve Elvina was, in fact, hiding a piece of bread for Gauthier! She ran toward the narrow street, ran to his hiding place to tell him something, to tell him what? She did not know. In the end she said nothing, because he was not alone. His brother, Robert, was with him. Robert looked a lot like Gauthier but taller and stronger. He was dressed like a knight, with a sword at his side, and he thanked Elvina for having looked after Gauthier so well.

"His eyes are less swollen, thanks to your ointment. But listen: the eclipse has terrified the Crusaders. This morning they are rushing about in all directions. They seem to have gone mad. Some are accusing the Jews of having caused the moon to disappear, and they are talking about stopping the Jews from ever doing it again. You can imagine what that means. I ran here to tell Gauthier, so now you must go quickly and warn your people."

While Robert was speaking, Gauthier bit into the bread and chewed it hungrily. His eyes were shining. *You see, we too have kept our word!* proclaimed the expression on his face.

"But they've seen you, and they've seen me, too. They know you're hiding here." Elvina stayed just long enough to whisper this warning.

Now she is running once again, this time toward the synagogue, where the men are finishing morning prayers.

Mazal, Mazal, don't bother with me anymore. I don't deserve it! I have been useless! Go help my father's Mazal instead. My father will need both of you to protect him. He has gone to Peter the Hermit to give him the money the Jews have collected. Dieulesault and Simonet are with him; they are both strong, but what can three men do against thousands?

When I arrived in front of the synagogue the men had finished saying morning prayers. My father had already left. My grandfather saw me crying. He stroked my hair and said soothingly, "The moment we were talking about has come. The eclipse can only turn the Crusaders against us. We have two solutions left: money and prayer."

Then someone told my grandfather that he was needed in the synagogue, and he ordered me to go home quickly — and to stay there.

Mazal, can all these events have been my fault? Could I be responsible for the eclipse that has upset the Crusaders so and made them hate us Jews even more? My father is at their mercy! Mazal, Mazal, I beg you, rush to the aid of Judah ben Nathan!

XXII

azal, if I'm talking to you, it is only out of habit, and also to remind you that to-day you should forget about me. Instead, please help my father's Mazal. Both of you, be guides to Judah ben Nathan. Make sure he takes the right paths, that is, not the same ones as the Crusaders. They are strangers to our region, so they prefer to keep to the main roads.

For my part, I've vowed not to eat anything until my father returns. How could I possibly eat? The idea that I may somehow be responsible for the dangers fac-ing my father and his companions chokes me like a necklace that is too tight.

Mazal, surely you know that my father sometimes has his head in the clouds. In case you don't already know it, I'm telling you. He can't tell one field from another or the difference between two roads. Mazal, make him follow Simonet's advice, because Simonet knows the countryside much better than he does.

"Elvina, who are you talking to?" asks Precious.

"Nobody. I'm talking to myself."

"Instead of daydreaming, help me wring out the tablecloth!" Precious replies impatiently.

Elvina whispers, "Good-bye for now, Mazal. I will say no more. I don't want to distract you from your mission."

Since morning, the servants have been sweeping the floor thoroughly under Precious's supervision. They have made sure that not the slightest crumb, wisp of straw, or cobweb remains. They have shaken out the blankets, beaten the pillows, and polished the wooden chests and wardrobes until the wood shone. They have cleaned the kitchen utensils, scrubbing saucepans and rubbing away at the metal latches on the chests.

Precious and Elvina have washed the white cloth that will be spread on the table the following evening for the Sabbath. May it please the Almighty to bring back Judah and Miriam, so that the Sabbath may see the whole of Solomon's family reunited!

The usual daytime noises come in through the open door and windows: the bleating of ewes about to give birth, children crying, a peddler shouting his wares, and birds calling. Neighbors drop by, one after the other, amazed to see this spring-cleaning. After all, there is still a full month to go before Passover!

But they know that for Precious and Elvina all this activity is a way of keeping their minds busy while they wait for the return of Miriam and Judah. The neighbors offer encouragement, saying that at least the weather is fine, so the roads will be dry, that the three men do not have far to go, and that, in any case, the Crusaders have no reason to make trouble for Jews who are giving them money.

As for Elvina, never in her whole life has a day seemed so long.

She has polished the beautiful Sabbath lamp herself, as well as Solomon's and Judah's spice boxes. The servants have peeled turnips and leeks and set them to boil with onions, chervil, and eggs. Such a meal will indeed comfort Judah ben Nathan when he returns.

When the bell of the neighboring church rings out midday, they all hurry to the door, dusters and brooms in hand, as if the ringing bell would somehow bring them the news they are waiting for so anxiously. But the courtyard remains empty. The chickens strut and peck around as usual, the sky grows paler, the wind blows colder, and the yellow light of the sinking sun's rays dances on the newly burnished metalwork.

A horse's neighing echoes in the street, and there is the sound of hooves. The youngest servant cries out to Precious, "Mistress! A group of horsemen is stopping at our house! I think they are Jewish merchants. Their saddlebags are filled to bursting, and one of the riders is a woman!"

Before Miriam has even dismounted or pushed back her hood, old Zipporah has recognized her. "It's the mistress!" she cries.

All the women run toward the traveler, gathering around her and unfolding the woolen scarf that covers her nose and mouth. Elvina sees her mother's face, white with exhaustion, her cheekbones and forehead black with dust. But her eyes are shining with joy. Miriam stretches out her arms to Elvina and hugs her tightly. Then, still holding her, Miriam stands back and exclaims, "How pale you are, my child! Your hair is disheveled, and your dress is covered with stains!"

She has already started to fix one of Elvina's braids. Pulling her daughter's ear, Miriam pinches the lobe between her thumb and forefinger. She says, "Tomorrow I'll pierce your ears to put in the golden earrings that your Aunt Yochebed has sent you. They're in my purse. You'll see how pretty they are."

Elvina feels as though she has become a child again. Her mother pats and strokes her, licks a finger, and rubs a smudge off her cheek, exactly as she used to do when Elvina was small. "Why are you so dirty? What have you been doing?" asks Miriam.

Elvina breathes in her mother's familiar smell. They take each other's hands as if they were about to start dancing. "We've been cleaning both houses. Anyway," retorts Elvina, "you should take a look at yourself. Your forehead is all scratched."

"A branch hit me as we were riding through the forest. We were going fast, and I didn't duck in time. But you haven't told me about your friend Tova and her baby. How are they? Later we'll go visit them."

Miriam and Elvina laugh and hug each other and talk about their plans.

Soon a crowd has gathered in front of Solomon ben Isaac's house. Someone hurries off to tell him the news, and he drops everything and comes running at once. He is beaming, radiant with happiness at seeing his daughter safe and sound! Samuel and Yom Tov, who have been allowed out of school, follow close on Solomon's heels. The neighbors press around Miriam, and one after the other, they throw their arms around her and rejoice. Even the cat rubs himself against the hem of her skirt.

Miriam kisses her father; then she turns to Samuel. "Your father, Meir ben Samuel, sends his blessing; your mother is in good health. Your brother, Isaac, and sister Fleurdelis and little Hannah are all well, may God protect them."

Precious has already started giving orders, and the servants get busy. They bring out pitchers of water and towels so the travelers can wash their hands. On the table in the dining room jugs of wine and goblets are set down. There is a pot full of steaming cooked vegetables with bread and cheese as well as apples, nuts, dried figs, and honey cakes. What a spread! Nothing is too fine to celebrate the return of Solomon's eldest daughter. He has invited the four merchants who have brought Miriam home to come in and eat. Neighbors have taken charge of leading the horses to the stables and feeding them.

Elvina sits on one side of Miriam and Precious on the other. They watch Miriam dunking her bread into the soup as if they had never seen her do it before! Zipporah and the two other servants can't stop touching her, as if to make sure that she is really here in the flesh. Miriam shakes them off laughing: "You're crushing me! Let me eat; I'm hungry. We've been on the road since dawn, and we only stopped once in the forest at midday."

Little by little, the table grows silent. Miriam turns to Solomon ben Isaac and says, "My father must certainly have wondered what I was doing traveling the day after an eclipse."

"I imagine that my son-in-law Meir ben Samuel didn't allow you to leave without considering the matter carefully," replies Solomon, smiling.

In reply, Miriam explains, "This morning, Meir ben Samuel woke up before the cock crowed. He had dreamed that the moon was setting on the horizon, only to disappear in a torrential river. He immediately recited the verses: 'Behold, I direct peace towards Jerusalem, as a river. . . .' and 'The moon shall be confounded and the sun shall be ashamed.'"

"And how did he interpret this dream?" asks Solomon.

"He explained that the river represented peace," Miriam continues. "As for the moon, those who worship her will be brought to grief, for she is nothing but a luminary obeying the Almighty's will. From this interpretation of his dream, Meir ben Samuel concluded that God would not let the Crusaders mistreat the Jews using the moon as an excuse. He also thought that the troops of Peter the Hermit would soon be on their way and would leave us in peace. After that, Meir ben Samuel told the *shamash* to inform the merchants that it was safe for them to set out."

The four men, who are eating and drinking in silence, nod their approval. The eldest says, "We were quite ready, because we were in a hurry to leave. Our road is long; it takes us all the way to Flanders."

Elvina turns toward Miriam. "Weren't you frightened?"

"Of course I was," replies Miriam, "but I so badly wanted to go home! And if your uncle's dream was good enough for the merchants, it was good enough for me! We were on horseback, traveling quickly, so it was less dangerous. We went through the forest using paths that the Crusaders don't know. We didn't meet a soul."

Next to Elvina, Solomon ben Isaac laughs with his gentle, mischievous chuckle; it is the way he used to chuckle. "See how my granddaughter can't believe her ears! Didn't you know that you get your courage from your mother . . . not to mention your passion for taking risks?"

Suddenly Miriam sits up and her eyes travel around the room. "Where is Judah ben Nathan? Where is my husband? Haven't they told him I'm back?"

Everyone stops speaking. There is silence. Then Solomon answers, "Judah ben Nathan has gone to take the money collected by the Jews to Peter the Hermit. Your husband will be back before nightfall."

XXIII

Solomon has headed back to the synagogue, taking with him the four merchants. They will be given lodging for the night with local families.

Miriam shivers. She orders the servants to relight the fire, for Judah ben Nathan will certainly need hot water when he comes home. She sends Zipporah across the courtyard to the other house to fetch clean clothes and a blanket in case he might be cold.

She has kept Samuel and Yom Tov with her, although they wanted to get back to school. She inspects their eyes, mouths, and noses. "Breathe out; put out your tongues. Show me your fingers; good, only a little frostbite on Samuel's hands. I'll make you a dressing for them. It will be gone in three days."

Samuel protests, "But I won't be able to write!"

"Don't worry. You only need the dressings at night when you're asleep."

Miriam's tone is firm and reassuring. It is the voice Elvina knows so well that she believes she is hearing it even when her mother is away. Elvina can imitate this voice herself whenever circumstances require it. But today she perceives the anxiety in her mother's tone; she is talking more than usual, and more quickly.

"Now let me see your heads! Look at these mops! Didn't you ever wash while I was away? You're full of head lice! Didn't Elvina delouse you, not even once?"

The boys shake their heads and look knowingly at each other. Yom Tov whistles through his teeth. "Apparently, she had better things to do!"

"Elvina, come here!" calls Miriam.

Elvina approaches, dragging her feet. Never have they felt so leaden. Her head is spinning. She is a little weak. She has watched the others eat without swallowing a mouthful herself. Nobody noticed, for all eyes were upon her mother.

Miriam appears to be passionately interested in the boys' head lice. "Look at the colonies of vermin they have here! We'll have to give them a rinse! Elvina," she orders, "you will mix some alcohol of aniseed with vinegar!"

Elvina pretends to look at the brown and red bunches of hair her mother is showing her, but a lump forms heavily in her throat. *If only my mother knew! If she knew that I might be partly to blame for any harm that may have come to Judah ben Nathan this very day — and, if he has been harmed, we will learn all too soon!*

"Elvina, have you lost your tongue?" Miriam asks anxiously. "I can hardly recognize you; what's the matter? You seem worried about something; what is it? Answer me."

Elvina doesn't have time to answer, for just at that moment a woman arrives, exclaiming, "Miriam! So they were telling the truth! You really are here! I wanted to see for myself!" The newcomer is a rich widow, a childhood friend of Miriam and Yochebed. She has walked into the house without knocking. She rushes up to Miriam and hugs her. The woman smells of perfume and is wearing a beautiful head scarf with a snow-white wimple. Embracing Precious and Elvina, she plies Miriam with questions about the health of Yochebed and her children, Meir ben Samuel's business, and the Crusaders at Ramerupt. Miriam pulls up an armchair and asks the visitor to sit down, which she does without even stopping to draw breath.

"So these dreadful Crusaders didn't hurt you?"

Miriam replies, "They have set themselves up in barns and fields. You have to admit that they live peacefully enough. They took a few sheep and a donkey from my brother-in-law, but they didn't actually hurt anyone. It seems they are in a hurry to set off for Jerusalem."

The two friends endlessly exchange news. Elvina listens to them with one ear only. The other is straining toward the window and the street outside. Precious serves mulled wine. Above the rooftops the sky gradually grows dimmer, becoming pale pink and then silver. The first star comes out. Elvina can barely distinguish the faces in the room. The boys have made themselves scarce.

A servant has placed two lamps on the table and begins to light them. Miriam, always so polite and gentle with the servants as with everyone else, suddenly yells, "Since when do we light the lamps in broad daylight? How stupid can you be? Can't you see the sun is shining?"

The servant bursts into sobs and then Miriam does the same. Her friend gets up and holds her comfortingly, motioning the servant to take the lamps away, saying, "Night has not yet fallen; we have plenty of time."

Then there is silence, and the sky, despite what Miriam and her friend have just said, grows even darker, and a second star appears.

But suddenly there is the sound of voices from the street and a shout from Zipporah.

"Here comes the master! Here is Judah ben Nathan! Thank heaven! He looks hot; he must have been walking fast!"

Miriam jumps up, sidesteps her friend, pushes the servants out of the way, and, followed by Precious and Elvina, runs toward the courtyard, where her husband has already arrived. Samuel and Yom Tov are leaping around Judah, welcoming him noisily like a couple of puppies.

He smiles quite cheerfully at Miriam. "As soon as I entered the town I was told you had returned." He looks tired, but only because of his long walk. He has pushed back his cape, and his face glows with color.

For the second time that day, Solomon ben Isaac is running home. He heads straight for his son-in-law and takes him by the shoulders. "I'm glad to see you, my son. Now I can tell you how worried I was!"

They have brought Judah ben Nathan everything he needs to wash his hands and face. He sits down at the table, and they serve him a good meal, while

Miriam pours out wine. Elvina has never seen her father eat and drink with such relish. The whole family is standing around him, eager to hear everything he has to say.

Solomon ben Isaac is giving Judah time to get his strength back, but not for a second does he take his eyes off his son-in-law's face.

"From the way you look, I suppose that your mission went off without a hitch. Tell us all about it, my son; you can see we're dying to hear."

So Judah tells his story.

"As soon as we had left the outskirts of town, a small group of Crusaders joined us. They were polite young men from good families, judging from the way they spoke. They weren't like those brutal ruffians who steal sheep and terrify the villagers. One of these young men, a lad called Robert —"

Elvina lets out a little gasp. Judah stops speaking and looks at her. He raises his eyebrows, then continues.

"So, this lad, Robert, said that he would escort us to Peter the Hermit's headquarters. I was too busy thinking about our mission to wonder where this unexpected help had come from. I just thanked young Robert and also the Almighty. We walked along the fields and then entered the forest. There a band of villains fell upon us. They were armed with sticks and knives. They were yelling that the Jews had kidnapped a Christian boy by the name of Gauthier and that we would pay for this crime with our lives. Robert stood in front of us. He had his hand on his sword, and so did his companions. They looked impressive, I can tell you. The villains stopped shouting, and he spoke to them saying, 'Gauthier is my brother. He was not kidnapped; he ran away. And he was cared for and fed in the Jewish neighborhood. These three Jews are thus entitled to our gratitude and our protection.'"

While Judah speaks they all hold their breath.

"Then what?" asks Samuel.

"Then he told them that we were on a mission to see Peter the Hermit and he asked them, or rather ordered them, to join us."

Solomon asks what they were all burning to know.

"And did you see Peter the Hermit in person?"

"Yes. We gave him the purse and the letters addressed to our brothers in Germany. He looked at the letters and asked us to translate them. I did, and assured him that the Jewish communities in Germany would make sure he obtained provisions and money."

Samuel and Yom Tov shout out together, "Was Peter the Hermit on his donkey?"

Judah gives a half smile, looking slightly annoyed. "I hope that you, too, aren't going to ask me if that beast has the gift of language! I didn't see the donkey. His master was sitting on a pile of wood. Even Peter the Hermit's donkey must need a rest now and then!"

For a while, nobody speaks. The neighbors who have come to congratulate Judah ben Nathan leave. The night is falling. Everyone wants to hurry home before it gets completely dark.

Judah has finished his meal. "Who on earth, in our neighborhood, could have given shelter to that Gauthier?" he asks. "What Jew would dare take such a risk and put the whole community in danger? And why do such a thing?" He pauses for a moment before concluding, "What I do know is that whoever he was, I owe him my life."

A hush falls over the room. Elvina is pressing both hands on the table to support herself. Her mother looks at her anxiously. "What's the matter, my child? You look as if you're going to faint!"

Solomon puts his arms around Elvina's shoulders and speaks directly to Judah. "Judah, my son, now it is time for you to learn what I have known since yesterday."

Judah's eyes dart from Solomon to Elvina. He has grown very pale. Elvina thinks she will die, fall down and die, right here, right now. Miriam comes close and puts her arms around Elvina's waist to hold her up. Solomon continues, "Your daughter has a generous heart. Because of that, she takes risks. It was the Lord's will that, for the second time, her impetuousness be rewarded."

Judah puts his head in his hands. "My daughter is crazy! She hid a Crusader?"

Elvina throws herself into her mother's arms and sobs. She buries her face in Miriam's shoulder; she is sure she is about to die. Then she hears a voice somewhere above her.

"Elvina saved your life. You've just said so; we heard you!"

These words have come from Miriam! Miriam is actually contradicting Judah ben Nathan! Elvina is so amazed that she raises her head.

Miriam pushes her daughter, shaking with hiccups and sobs, toward Judah. Judah places his hand on his daughter's head and leaves it there. No one says a word. Even Samuel and Yom Tov are quiet. Elvina calms down, sniffs, and wipes her face with her sleeve. She doesn't quite understand what is happening. In fact, nothing is happening. It is a moment of extraordinary peace. It seems to her that her father is swallowing hard; then, in an emotional and solemn voice, which Elvina has never heard him use before, Judah says, "Blessed be the Lord." Then he looks at Miriam, and in his usual ironic tone he continues, "What a strange daughter the Almighty has sent us!"

XXIV

Two weeks have gone by since these frightening events shook our whole community and my family. Tomorrow there will be a new moon. In Troyes, we will celebrate it even more joyfully than usual, because the Crusaders have finally gone away. In two weeks' time the moon will be full and we shall celebrate Passover. We will remember that the Almighty led us out of Egypt, where we were slaves. And we will also remember that He didn't allow the Crusaders to harm us. Now we will pray for our brothers in the German communities.

Peter the Hermit and his troops are making their way to Germany. I have been told that the roads are crowded with people. They form an endless and uninterrupted line of men and women, though I haven't seen them myself. I am not allowed to walk out of the town. I must say that I miss my conversations with Gauthier. I hope that isn't a sin!

One evening, as I was serving Judah ben Nathan his meal, he motioned me to stay by him. He looked at me with his ironic smile and said, "I have been given a message for my daughter."

I was amazed. Who would be bold enough to use Judah ben Nathan as a messenger! And with a message for me! I said nothing. He continued, "It's about your young protégé, Gauthier. His brother asked me to tell you that Gauthier obtained permission to go and study in the monastery. His uncles finally gave in to his determination. He thought you'd be pleased to hear it." My father added, "I greatly fear that once he has studied long enough, he may use his knowledge against the Jews, to make fools of them and ridicule their faith. And I can tell you that Solomon ben Isaac would agree with me."

I knew better than to answer back, but at the bottom of my heart I was sure that all his life Gauthier would defend the Jews and protect them in memory of me. Sometimes when I think of him, I see him again crying for his mother, and I cry a little, too.

There are two others who are crying today: Naomi and Rachel, for they are going back to their village tomorrow. Why are they crying? Because I will no longer be able to make them read every day as I have done until now.

"We will no longer be students," they say miserably. "We will become just ordinary girls again." And they start crying.

I told them to come every week for the Sabbath. "We won't be able to write on the Sabbath," I said. "But every week I'll copy a passage from the Bible for you. We will read it and translate it so that you can learn it. I'll copy longer and longer passages. You will still be my students."

"Promise?" they said at the same time.

"I promise," I replied. They got out the tablets I gave them. I copied out all the letters so they could practice when they returned home.

That afternoon, my grandfather, Solomon ben Isaac, came and asked my mother if he could take me for a little walk. There was laughter in his eyes, and Miriam's eyes were also laughing. We walked toward the school.

On the way, I reminded Solomon ben Isaac that when I was little he always used to take advantage of our walks to teach me something.

He smiled and said, "Tomorrow will be the new

moon; you'll rest and have a nice time with your mother and your girlfriends. Why is that?"

I knew he was going to talk to me about the women's special day of rest, but I said nothing.

He smiled, because my silence did not fool him. Then he took on the tone of voice he uses when he is about to tell one of his favorite stories. "I'm going to tell you what my old master used to say. 'When the Jews had just left Egypt and were wandering in the desert, they asked Aaron to build the golden calf so they could worship it. They started by gathering together all their jewelry to be melted down to make the golden calf. But the women refused to give up their earrings, bracelets, and necklaces. As a reward, the Lord decreed that the first day of each month would be a day of rest for women, old and young alike.'" My grandfather added, "Tomorrow I want to see you having fun and resting, according to our tradition."

We had arrived in front of the school and my grandfather sent a student to fetch Obadiah. Obadiah came out. He looked only at my grandfather, as if I were not standing there beside him.

"Obadiah ben Moyses, here is a student I highly recommend whenever her duties as future mistress of a house leave her the time to come and listen to you," my grandfather said, his eyes sparkling.

Obadiah blushed. He gave a little bow but still did not look at me; then he went back inside the school. Grandfather and I left. Solomon had asked me to write a few letters for him. I noticed that he stooped a little and, when he wasn't looking at me, his eyes were full of sorrow. I took his hand. "My grandfather looks sad," I said.

"I won't hide from you that I am worried about our German brothers. My old fellow students and their families live in Worms and Mainz. It was God's wish that our community be spared. We pray every day that He show the same compassion to our German brothers." He pinched my cheek. "You are too young to be sad. When I look at you, my heart grows lighter. Do you realize that your old grandfather is looking forward to dancing at your wedding? Don't make him wait too long!"

My wedding? Mazal, did you hear that?

Dear, dear Mazal!

Afterword

This story takes place in the town of Troyes (pro-nounced "twah") in the region of Champagne, in France, during the spring of 1096. Troyes was a medium-sized town, with a population of three or four thousand people, including a community of about four hundred Jews. Many were craftspeople, but most of them had vineyards and produced wine used by both Jews and Christians.

Solomon ben Isaac was born in Troyes in 1040. He studied for several years in the great Jewish academies of Mainz and Worms, in Germany. He then returned to Troyes, where he taught in his own academy, or *yeshivah*, which became very famous.

Solomon realized that Jews were forgetting Hebrew, the language of the Bible, and also Aramaic, the language of the Talmud, so that it was becoming increasingly difficult for them to read their holy books.

His precise and detailed commentaries soon became so famous, that Jews made copies of them to take wherever they traveled and settled and wouldn't dream of studying without them. This is still true today. Both the Bible and Talmud are published with his commentary printed in smaller characters below or alongside the text.

Solomon ben Isaac died in Troyes in 1105. He is known under the name of Rashi, which is the acronym of Rabbi Shlomo Yitzhaki, his Hebrew name.

Solomon ben Isaac had no sons, but he had three daughters, Miriam, Yochebed, and Rachel, and several grandchildren. Two of his grandsons became particularly famous rabbis and commentators: the oldest of Yochebed's sons, Samuel ben Meir, known as Rashbam, and the youngest, Jacob ben Meir, known as Rabbenu Tam.

His granddaughter Elvina was highly regarded during her lifetime for her knowledge and wisdom, but she did not leave a written work for us to read.

In the early months of 1096, the first Crusade began. The pope, Urban II, had called on Christians to march to the Holy Land and conquer the Christian Holy Places (among them the tomb of Jesus) and take them back from the Muslims.

The Crusaders first gathered in France. Then, their numbers in the thousands, they went on to Germany and then farther east, attracting more and more people as they progressed toward Jerusalem. They were called Crusaders because they sewed or attached crosses to their outer garments.

The Crusaders, who went through Troyes, led by Peter the Hermit, did not harm the Jewish population. But when they reached the German cities of Mainz, Worms, and Speyer in May 1096 they were joined by more brutal and more fanatical troops who were very hostile to the Jews. Thousands of Jews met death at their hands. Solomon ben Isaac's last years were much saddened by the loss of many of his old friends in Mainz and Worms.

Glossary

Ark: The Holy Ark or Ark of the Covenant is a chest that contained the Tablets of the Law. Above the Ark, the two cherubim stood with their protective wings outstretched. The Ark is the symbol of the covenant between the Hebrews and their God.

Bar Mitzvah: This means, literally, "son of the commandment." Bar Mitzvah celebrates the age of religious majority, when a boy turns thirteen and is responsible for his actions. In the eyes of Jewish law, he is considered to be a man. In current time, girls celebrate their Bat Mitzvah, which means "daughter of the commandment."

Beth Midrash: This means "House of Study" and is the school that is attached to the synagogue.

Havdalah: The ritual marking the end of the Sabbath.

Leviticus: The third of the first five books of the Bible, which make up the Torah.

Mazal (mah-*zahl*): A guardian angel. According to Jewish belief, every human being has a Mazal to plead his or her cause in heaven. In the Talmud and Midrash, *Mazal* also means "constellation of the zodiac," "constellation at one's birth," and "destiny." And it is commonly associated with luck, as in "mazel tov," which means "good luck."

Mazzikim: Evil spirits. Certain legends say they are souls of the wicked transformed into demons as punishment. They have several things in common with angels: They have wings and fly from one end of the earth to the other, they can see the future, and of course they are invisible.

Parashah: The Torah is divided into fifty-four parts, each of which is called a *parashah*. Each Saturday in the synagogue, the parashah of the week is read.

Passover: A festival commemorating the liberation of the Hebrews from slavery under the pharaohs and the Hebrews' flight from Egypt. Under the leadership of Moses, the Hebrews were guided through the Sinai Desert for forty years, on their way to the Promised Land.

Purim: The festival commemorating the Jewish victory in Persia over those who wanted to massacre them. The Scroll of Esther, one of the books in the

Bible, tells how Esther, the Jewish wife of the Persian king Ahasuerus, saved the Jews. She was helped and guided by her Uncle Mordecai and managed to foil the plot of Haman, the king's wicked vizier.

The day of Purim is one of great rejoicing: There is plenty of food and drink, and people give one another presents and wear disguises. The carnival atmosphere is supposed to show that nothing is really what it seems and that the true meaning of events is often hidden.

Sabbath: The day of rest. In Jewish households, the Sabbath begins at sundown on Friday evening and lasts until nightfall on Saturday. It is a joyful occasion; the house must be cleaned, the table set, and the meal prepared in advance, so that the whole day may be given over to rest, prayer or study, conversations with friends, or walks.

The Sabbath ends with Havdalah, a ceremony marking the separation between the Sabbath and everyday life. Wine, perfume, and light receive a special blessing.

Tabernacle (Mishkan in Hebrew): A portable temple built by the Hebrews during their wanderings in the Sinai Desert.

Talmud: The interpretation and elaboration of what is called the oral law by rabbis who discuss its meaning. The Talmud was written in Hebrew and Aramaic in Jerusalem and Babylon between the third and fifth century CE (Common Era).

Temple: The First Temple was constructed by King Solomon in Jerusalem in the tenth century BCE (Before the Common Era). The Ark was kept in a part of the Temple called the Holy of Holies, a place where only the High Priest was allowed to enter and only on the Day of Atonement. The First Temple was destroyed in 586 BCE. The Second Temple was built in 516 BCE and was destroyed by the Romans in 70 CE. One wall of the Second Temple still remains, and it is known today as the Wailing Wall.

Tent: The tent was also called the Tent of Meeting, because it was where God "met with man" or revealed himself to man. This tent, which was made from eleven large goat-hair curtains, covered the tabernacle.

Torah: The root of this word means "to teach." The Torah is the scroll that contains the first five books of Moses, which are Genesis, Exodus, Leviticus, Numbers, and Deuteronomy.

This English-language translation was edited
by Dianne Hess and designed by Elizabeth B. Parisi.
The cover was designed by Steve Scott, with
a photograph by Larry Rostant.
The art for the title page was created by
Bagram Ibatoulline, using acryl-gouache, gouache,
and watercolor. The photograph used beneath the
type on the back cover is of a wooden book cover
from around the time of Rashi. Thanks to the
Bibliotheque Municipale de Reims, France, for
allowing us to use the image. The text was set
in Centaur, a typeface designed in 1914 by
Bruce Rogers.

Sylvie Weil grew up in France and earned degrees in classics and French literature from the Sorbonne in Paris. She has taught in several universities, first in France, then in the United States.

Ms. Weil encountered Rashi, the eminent commentator on the Bible and the Talmud, while studying the Bible in Hebrew. His commentaries revealed what a generous, down-to-earth man he was, and she wrote a book about him for adults. But when it was finished, she couldn't bear to leave him behind. So she wrote a novel about his family from the point of view of his real-life granddaughter, Elvina.

Ms. Weil makes her home in both Paris and New York City.

Gillian Rosner has translated many award-winning books for children. Both *Secret Letters from 0 to 10* and *A Book of Coupons* by Susie Morgenstern were named Mildred L. Batchelder Honor Books for translation and ALA Notable Children's Books. *A Book of Coupons* was also named a 2004 IBBY Honor Book for a work translated in the United States. She lives in the South of France.